Five O'Clock Shadow

and other stories

For

John and Maggie Sweeney

Contents

Editor's Note	i	
Introduction	iii	
Five O'Clock Shadow	1	Kathryn Hughes
The Neighbor	9	Julia Asher
Drowned Boy	23	Kevin Parry
The Lobster Shift	33	Eleanor Flegg
Little Stevie Augers In	45	Robert Grindy
Ahmad's Teeth	59	Sami Moukaddem
Volunteers	69	Audrey Thomas
Teller of Tales	79	Lisa Steppe
Swift Water	87	Melissa Gaskill
Mrs Purvis	99	Robin Winick
Making History	111	Morag McIntyre Hadley
Skate Blades	121	Celia Bryce
History of a Vagrant	137	Sylvia Baker
All the Good Times Too	147	Ian Baker
Toppling Lorna	163	Rebecca Lisle
Cloud Shadows	173	Frank Cossa
Headline News	187	Pansy Billingsly

Editor's Note

One of the gratifications of running the Fish Short Story Prize is to witness writers featured in the anthology go on to full-length publications of their own. In the last year alone Fish has published books by three of those writers – *Altergeist* by Tim Booth, *Small City Blues* by Martin Kelleher, and *The Woman Who Swallowed the Book of Kells* by Ian Wild. William Wall, Eamonn Sweeney, and Martin Malone have also had books published in the last year. More power to them all.

Congratulations to Kathryn Hughes, this year's winner, for her beautifully written story *Five O'Clock Shadow*, and to Kevin Parry and Julia Asher who share second prize. I hope they benefit from a week at Anam Cara Writer's and Artist's Retreat and a residential weekend at Dingle Writing Courses respectively.

The quality of entries to the competition remains very high indeed. This makes short-listing and judging extremely difficult, and means disappointment for many fine writers whose stories all but made it. On another day it may have been different for them. We set a high standard, and where objectivity is aimed at, it can never be achieved. These writers who made the short-list are named at the back of this book.

Kevin Parry and Rebecca Lisle appear in a Fish anthology for the second time, and are therefore not allowed to enter again. Well done to both of them. They have reached a standard of sufficient merit that disqualifies them and leaves the door open for others.

The Fish Art Prize was won by Dublin artist Aiden McDermott, and his painting *The Lost Coat* appears on the cover of this book. The £500 prize is sponsored by Vickery's Hotel, Bantry, Co. Cork, the hub of the Bantry Literary and Chamber Music Festival.

The editorial staff, Jula Walton, Yann and Claire Kelly-Hoffman, Jennifer Corcoran, and Frank O'Donovan, have worked with great diligence and commitment, and this book is here because of their efforts. Thanks to them, in particular Jula Walton, who did typesetting, cover design and much more. The independent judges were Dermot Bolger,

Julia Darling and William Wharton, and enormous credit is due for their selfless work and genuine interest in helping emerging writers. Thank you!

The last year has also seen the birth of the Literary Fringe to the West Cork Chamber Music Festival. The launch of last year's anthology kicked off the festival in Bantry House. This anthology will be similarly launched and readings and workshops will continue for the week. Jennifer Johnston, Dermot Healy, Aiden Higgins, Paula Meehan, Tony Curtis, Pat Boran and Antonia Logue are among those who have participated. Michael Hartnett died last year, he was an honorary patron of the Literary Fringe, and a participant on two notable occasions. He was as much loved as his poetry was admired. He was nature's finest. He will be missed.

Introduction

It's interesting that there are not more short stories in circulation. In these fast times when attention span is allegedly shortening, and the sound-bite has taken hold, why are the reading public not queuing up to buy the latest batch of short stories? Particularly at airports and stations, where one would think a book of short reads would be entirely preferable to a several hundred page blockbuster? A well known novelist said recently on a TV programme that many who buy her books read them four miles high and only the first 60 pages. It's like the eyes are bigger than the stomach – ordering a 16 oz steak and eating only eight and you haven't touched the chips. But at least you know what you are getting. Like a trip to MacDonalds. It's safe. Anywhere in the world you can be served the same bland fare. No matter that you might not eat all of it, or that however much you do eat you'll still be hungry in an hour. There are no surprises.

And that's where the good short story differs. It may shock, surprise, dazzle, leave you high and dry, out on a limb and hanging. It might change the way you look at something, the way you think. You don't know what you are buying, what you are letting yourself in for. I sometimes feel like issuing a health warning with the Fish Anthology – *these stories may seriously damage your outlook* - The seventeen stories in this book come from all over the place, but they have in common their originality. Here is the view of writers who see the world in their unique way, and have the imagination, talent, and the courage to refine it into that most surprising of all art forms – the short story.

Clem Cairns

Kathryn Hughes

Winner of the Fish Short Story Prize

Kathryn Hughes is an MFA candidate in the writing program at the School of the Art Institute of Chicago. Her work has been published in and won various awards from a number of literary journals including River Styx, Glimmer Train, Creative Nonfiction and The Benningham Review. Currently she's working on her thesis, a collection of short stories including 'Five O'Clock Shadow.' Kathryn lives in Kenilworth Illinois with her two daughters.

Five O'Clock Shadow

Kathryn Hughes

February 13, 1950

What if you hadn't been born, if your father hadn't pressed your mother to try one last time for a girl, if she'd said *No more, five's enough. Enough babies.* Perhaps you would have been something else. Maybe Man O' War winning 20 out of 21 starts and voted The Greatest Horse of the First Half of the Century, or his groom, or the currycomb that smoothed his gleaming, sorrel hide smelling musky and fine; and that would have been enough. Or you could have been one of his trophies or another prize, the Nobel Prize, the one for Literature for the most distinguished literary work of an idealistic nature, a heavy gold medal in Faulkner's sure hands. Or if you hadn't been a little girl, you might have been an American soldier, just a kid really, killed on Korean turf. Or Truman's pen or simply his signature approving development of the hydrogen bomb, a boy and his toys. Instead, imagine being warm celluloid accepting the image of Gary Cooper all spaniel eyes, soft mouth and friendly persuasion; or his crisp shirt next to him or his suspenders, embracing him; or you could've been one of Hogey Carmichael's cigarettes, musical embers, or the keys on his honky-tonk, extensions of himself. But now you're getting carried away. Because what you really were, all you were, was Daddy's early Valentine.

1

Words Beginning With 'P'

Princess. Pumpkin. Precious. Pussy Cat. Puppet. Not Pet. He saved that one for your mother. He wanted a little girl from the start, and had your room done all in pinks, eyelet lace skimming your four-poster bed, framing the windowpanes. He wanted you dressed in pinafores and petticoats, patent leathers on your stocking'd feet. He wanted ringlets in your hair, all ribboned in pastels. So he ordered your mother to schedule you for a perm; happily, you were allergic to the perming solution. An ambulance was called to the beauty parlor and you almost died. But your ponytail – long and straight and heavy with a little dip at the end, like a horse's – went unscathed. He wanted you to play girls' games. But except for your mother who, unlike most pets, never had time to play, there wasn't another female around for miles. So in an era before play dates and pre-schools, playing dolls you played alone. Playing dress-up, you talked to the mirror. Playing house was an empty, joyless place.

Instead you slipped into hand-me-down Levi's and high-tops and Fruit-o'-the-Loom t-shirts and, ponytail sticking out of your Cubs hat, followed your brothers like a chittering sparrow. Instead, tagging along, you played football in the fall; baseball in the spring and summer; basketball and hockey in the winter. Instead, you built a tree house and forts in the woods, climbed trees, rode bikes, skinned knees, bloodied noses. Instead you watched Gunsmoke and Dragnet, played cowboys and Indians, cops and robbers. For Christmas you asked for chaps, your own cap gun and holster, and a boy's Schwinn. Eventually, finally, your father began calling you by your actual name. *When* he called you. Which was less and then lesser still.

Five O'Clock Shadow

You hardly ever see Gregory Peck anymore and when you do he has aged so, with a mane of white hair and bushy black eyebrows, looking more Moby Dick than Roman Holiday. But he's kept his shape and that voice, that voice. And integrity to boot I mean, how many of us think he actually *was* Atticus Finch? You used to think that your father looked just like him, though you feel now that you know the actor better than your own dad and probably because being a fan of old movies you've seen

2

more of him speaking of which: in The Snows of Kilimanjaro, Peck's fluid voice like velvet thunder rumbles through his five o'clock shadow, giving timbre to literature. His character lies dying of gangrene in the hot Serengeti sun, even as a Negro steward fans him with a palm frond and Susan Hayward listens patiently to his feverish philosophical ramblings: *It's not dying, not in itself, that matters. It's dying of failure that leaves a bad taste in your mouth. How does a man...miss the boat?*

Your dad as it turned out needed to shave twice daily too, because though his distant eyes and deep voice no longer gave you the time of day, his whiskers did.

Still Life

He hunted with the ego and deliberation of Hemingway, though you never called him Papa. He'd been to Juneau and Hudson Bay and twice to Kenya, returning tanned, bearded, and arrogant. Your home was studded and mantled with his souvenirs, and skins and skulls intimidated visitors to his office.

Before your father invited clients and friends to the grounds for weekend days of hunting the woods and fields behind your house, celebrating after a lavish dinner with brandy and cigars, he always reserved opening day for his sons, planning beginning weeks in advance with procedure bordering on ritual. As a jealous observer you compared the solemnity of the preparation to that of your brothers' duties as altar boys. Assembly took place in the panelled study. Walnut walls lined in crucified hides of antelope and zebra soaked up voices like the hush in a chapel. Gun barrels were polished to tabernacle luster, bullets coddled like consecrated hosts. Trappings from Orvis were laid out like vestments.

The day finally came and you watched from your bedroom: hands and forehead pressed against the iced window, breath melting autumn frost into wet circles, they disappearing into the woods without you. Shivering, you slipped back into bed, pulling the quilt up over your head, breathing and re-breathing until you realized with some alarm that you might poison yourself with your own air. Flipping the coverlet down and away, you stared at the ceiling, inhaling cold, clean oxygen, your hands folded as if in prayer over your flannel-pajama'd heart. They had left you alone, to

3

your gender, in the dark. And you swallowed hard, longing to be out there with them, fighting the underbrush, exerting silence, a gun at your hip. All day the crackle of volleys bounced off of low-hung skies into your wondering earshot, and the birch trees outside your window bent in the wind like girls in a poem. Finally, between dusk and dark, these males would emerge from the thick trees, smelling of gunpowder, toting pheasant and hare hanging in limp suspension from taut lines, like a 17th century still life.

Communion

One year, the year you turned seven, you busied yourself all day with a plan and its execution. You erected an altar in the attic. Fortunately the top floor was accessible by a set of back stairs, not the receding kind that's pulled down with a cord from the ceiling. Fortunately for a scrawny kid trying to negotiate a card table up from the basement.

You knew by heart every word of the Latin Mass including the Requiem, which you found most beautiful with its minor chords. And when you sang it in the sloped ceiling'd space, your voice resonated, coming back to you, filling your ears with Sanctus, Sanctus, Sanctus. And yet your dreams of being a real altar boy were thwarted by dogma. Women knew their place in the Church and it wasn't up there next to Our Lord, the right hand Man to the Father. Women laundered and pressed vestments. The wearing and touching and turning bread into flesh was done entirely by men. The men made blood from wine by divine sanction, and gulped it from golden goblets polished by the women.

You blanketed the table with a starched white sheet, then copped two brass candlesticks from the buffet and the crucifix from the guest room. The wine supply being locked up in the cellar, you scavenged a half bottle of Chablis cooling in the fridge, and darkened it with beet juice. Finally, you dropped cinnamon and cloves pilfered from the spice cabinet into the candles' hot wax, filling the attic with your own brand of Benediction. For the altar railing you extended an old baby-gate between a couple of cardboard boxes marked Christmas Décor. With an ice pick you poked holes around an empty coffee can and wired it with a coat hanger over the bare bulb hanging from an eave so that the light it cast looked like stars.

You fashioned white wafers the size of quarters out of Wonder Bread and gingerly placed them in a shiny copper tureen stolen from the pantry. Finally, you stood back and, pleased with the overall effect, you christened your attic sanctuary The Chapel of the Sacred Heart. And under the halo of candlelight and flicker of starlight, the clean white sheet glowed as if possessed by the Holy Ghost Himself.

When Ellie Ironed

When Ellie ironed it was Tuesdays. Mondays she hung the linens perfumed by Clorox on the line to dry. Before she left for home in the evening, she'd spread them across the kitchen table and sprinkle them to just-damp with water, and wad them up in the plastic sheeting removed from the dry cleaning: bagged mounds to remain cool and damp in the basement refrigerator overnight. Like cellophaned sections of unassembled snowmen, filling the fridge in the overnight.

The next day she hauled them up to the kitchen where she had set up the ironing board and tuned in the radio to WVON (the Voice Of the Negro). And as little Etta James bellowed a tune and a d.j. with a smile in his saxophone of a voice jockeyed the discs from Record Row on South Michigan Avenue, Ellie misted cotton in Niagara and pressed to perfection the sheets, the pillowcases, and your daddy's boxer shorts.

She smoked Chesterfields and drank Co'-Cola from little green bottles. Her teeth were big and white despite the tobacco and soda pop, and her smile lit up the room, warming it like a fireplace in winter, sunshine in the spring. This was Tuesdays.

Alien

It appeared one Christmas morning. In an otherwise black basement it glowed beneath a single bright bulb capped by a tin shade centered over its breadth: a half-ton slab of slate wrapped in green felt and tied up with a red ribbon. A Brunswick pool table. You and your brothers stood in awe and plaid pajamas at the foot of the basement stairs; and on the wall a sextet of Wille Hoppe cue sticks hung like rifles behind the glass door of an oaken case. Your father ordered you, *Kathryn, get rid of the ribbon.* As you removed the velvet band, wrapping it tightly around your fist like a

5

scarlet set of brass knuckles, he blustered around the room bending the very light with his mass. Then as you watched and waited, he handed a cue stick to each of the boys, taking the last for himself. The smoke from his Pall Mall got into his eyes but he chalked his cue with one eye shut, as if it didn't matter. The ivory balls clopped inside a triangular wooden corral so perfectly that when he lifted the frame, not a ball flinched. He barrelled down, all aim and concentration, and quick as a lick sunk every ball into woven leather pockets. There was no hiding place under the hundred-watt Sylvania. Meanwhile, you and your brothers lingered half-embarrassed, lined up like little soldiers as in the cool concrete dark the table shimmered like a UFO in a June cornfield on a moonless night.

Lesson

Even now when you ride, you forego the crop and move your mount along with a cluck and tender nudge of stirrup, because you know the crop, and the sting of the crop; though there had been a time when you would go to the tack room, boot-heels soft thuds on wide, plank floors, just to smell the smells. Where dust lingered in a glance of sun streaming in through murky skylights, everything browns and olives and ambers but for your long hair, your hair glowing blonde like a lamp in a boudoir in a Merchant-Ivory film. You would touch the leather, wanting to call it your own because yes, you loved the smell of the tack room, and from the stalls the benign gaze of horses, and the soothing sounds of snort and munch as they scooped moist hay with their fleshy muzzles. But now and then this inner sanctum, this tack room, reeked of his bourbon breath, his clothes stale with tobacco, and the smell of fresh, young blood when he taught you a lesson you'd never forget.

Missing the Boat

On March 11th of the year you turned eight and he would have turned forty-four, he didn't wake up. One of your brothers found him stiffened and cold in his urine-stained twin bed as your mother, unawares, fried eggs and toasted toast and poured juice in the fluorescent-bright, linoleumed kitchen.

.   .   .

6

More frequently than times before, you find yourself slipping into a moment's melancholia at his passing too soon. More frequently in that, looking over your shoulder, you've already cleared that still-young, that same, his final age; though you must have done it on luck because it sure wasn't experience.

That sea grey death day you little realized its unforecasted overcasted double-crossing of him. You looked on mute and still as they wheeled him out of your life atop a squeaking gurney, under a white sheet. You only remember its effect on you – the relief only a badly losing team can know at the end of a long, long game; and on its tails that first ambivalent ache of many to know him other than in your dreams, to know him better, to know him at all. Because even then, sweet-child blind, you got an inkling of the utter finality of it all, the eternal dangling of so much unsaid, unresolved. And so you have settled instead for one-sided conversations as you lie in the night with himself, still not looking you in the eye or giving you the time of day.

Julia Asher

Joint second in the Fish Short Story Prize

Has a BFA in Painting from the School of Art Institute of Chicago. She is currently a fellow in The Pennsylvania Emerging Writers Programme. She has a fellowship to the Vermont Studio Centre in Johnson, Vermont, and to the Squaw Valley Community of Writers in California. She is working on a novel *Red's Never Fail*.

The Neighbor

Julia Asher

My little brother spent the morning stacking pallets. One by one against a chain link fence that separated us from a hunched and drunken old man we referred to as the Neighbor. Saturdays were the busiest. The phones stayed lit like downtown during Christmas.

George was on line one, he wanted to know if we had any mushrooms. He needed five boxes for the weekend. The big ones, not, the little ones. Make sure they're white and can we get them there fast?

Dell from Bischoff's was on line two. Where in the hell was his order? We told him any minute half a fuckin' hour ago and still, no tomatoes. What in the hell did we expect him to do? Wave a magic wand? Who did we think he was? Merlin the Fuckin' Magician?

Kroger Store Fifty Two was on line three. Did we have ten boxes of number four bananas and twenty boxes of the number sevens? If we did, then, send 'em quick. You only have five of the number fours? Well. Okay. Send five of the fours and twenty five of the sevens. You only have nineteen of the sevens? Okay. Send five of the fours, send nineteen of the sevens, and send six of the fives, if you have them. Otherwise, just send six of the sixes, and if you don't have them, send five of the fours and nineteen of the sevens. Got that? Okay. Talk to you on Monday. Have a good weekend.

It was the beginning of July and hotter than a pancake griddle. Trees stood silent. Leaves hung limp. Watermelons sold as fast as buy-one-get-

9

one-free cola. Back by the dumpsters sat two trucks, eighteen wheelers resting, filled to capacity with the big green bullets.

The office, which was nothing but a couple of old grey metal desks and black office chairs back by the bananas, was filled with people. Cooler doors opened. Cooler doors closed. The drivers were filling their orders. Hundreds of cardboard boxes sat, in the darkness of the dock, waiting to be loaded.

My father was making the coffee. He filled the dingy Mr. Coffee with water, scooped the brown grounds, placed the filter in the basket, and pushed the button. While he waited for the pot to fill, he rinsed out yesterday's cup, tossed in three creams, mixed in five sugars, and reached for the donuts.

"Goddamnit to hell, who ate the donuts? Jesus Fucking Christ. I just bought the motherfuckers. Is it too much to ask to have a fuckin' donut? I'm the one that bought the goddamned things. You people want donuts? Buy your own Goddamned donuts. Stay the hell away from mine. Jesus Christ. I can't have anything. Not even a Goddamned donut. Son of a Fuckin' Bitch. Bunch of no good leeches."

Every Saturday, my father stopped at Big Fred's Donuts. He said the only donuts worth buying were Big Fred's, that Fred had been in business for years, ever since 1952. He said that Fred might suck at fishing, but, one thing was for certain, the bastard sure knew how to make a donut. Each time we drove by, he honked and waved, and said, "That Son of a Bitchin' Fred must be doin' somethin' right, look at that new Cadillac."

My father picked up the box and glanced at the two lemon jelly rolls that sat abandoned in the corner. He looked at me, shook his head, tossed the box aside, and lit a cigarette.

"Where's your brother? You guys got a truck to unload. You gotta get those watermelons off by noon, that driver needs to get to Cincinnati. Go find Si Lee and tell him I said to help you. Don't be fuckin' around, and watch how you unload 'em, you guys toss those Goddamned melons around like you think they're fuckin' basketballs. And don't forget to count 'em. Castellini tries to screw me every chance he gets."

The driver was parked in the shade, sleeping. It was my job to wake him. The truck's big metal doors were propped open for ventilation. The watermelons were stacked from floor to ceiling. I walked the gravel, kicking stones.

I thought about watermelons. About how if they don't get enough air, they explode. Like popcorn in a frying pan. When it gets too hot, boom. The little pieces of yellow corn turn into fluffy white clouds. It's the same thing with watermelons, except, when they explode, there's pieces of red and green laying everywhere. I thought about how people pass trucks on the freeway and how they don't even know, inside some of those trucks, watermelons are exploding.

The Neighbor stood slumped and sunburnt. He was wearing blue Bermuda shorts. His hairy belly hung, like a half inflated blimp, just above the belt line. With his left hand, he held an empty beer bottle. With his right hand, he held the hose. He was watering his flowers. A garden filled with pinks and greens grew right outside his trailer. The hose was wrapped around his ankle, but, he didn't seem to notice.

"Hey, where you goin'?" The Neighbor asked as I walked by. "C'mon back here. Gotta question for ya. What's with you people? How many times I have ta tell ya ta quit hittin' my fence? How many times? You people think you own the place. Trucks pullin' in here all times of the day and night. That fence is mine. Keep your pallets to yourself, stay on your side, and there won't be a problem. I'm not gonna tell ya, again. You keep tippin' that fence, and we'll come to blows. That's a warnin' now. If ya know what's good for ya, you'll listen. Ya hear me? I'm a Marine. So, I won't have to tell ya who'll win. And tell that little smartass, I've got my eye on him. I ain't afraid of some little blondie punk. Pulls in here with that Camaro. Who's he think he is? Some kinda movie star or somethin'? Mr. Pretty Boy. Well. He won't be so pretty when I get done with him. You hear me? Just keep tippin' that fence."

By the time I reached the truck, the old man was silent. The hose was still wrapped around his ankle and the water was forming a puddle beneath his feet, but, it didn't seem to bother him, he was sitting at his picnic table, drinking. The truck was parked underneath the trees, the windows were rolled down, and the driver's feet were sticking out. I stepped onto the running board, hoisted myself up, and peeked in the window.

11

The radio was on low, Glen Campbell was singing "Witchita Lineman." "I'm a lineman for the county and I drive the main road...Searchin' in the sun for another overload...." A pack of unfiltered Camels sat on the passenger's seat and a couple of half eaten twinkies were sitting soggy on the dashboard. I didn't know how to wake the driver up. I considered blowing the horn. I thought about pulling his leg. I wondered if I should say, "Excuse me, sir, but, we need to unload the melons."

The truck smelled like cheeseburgers, cigarettes, and oil. My dad said that truckers lead lonely lives. That they're kinda like cowboys and their trucks are like horses. He said that outerspace and the Interstate are America's last frontiers. They reminded me of that television show, Bonanza. All those guys out on the prairie, roughing it. Eating beans and cornbread, sleeping on the ground, building little fires, trying to stay warm.

"Hey, Goddamnit, what in the hell are you doin'?" My father stood near the pallets, watching. "C'mon, wake the son of a bitch up. Let's get goin'. Didn't I tell you that that guy needs to get to Cincinnati? And that Moran wants to look at those melons? Where the hell are you, in la-la land, or, something?"

I peeked at the driver. His neck was crooked. I bet when he woke up, he was going to have a headache. I was thinking about his headache when his toe hit the volume button. "And I need you more than want you and I want you for all time....And the Witchita Lineman is still on the line." The trucker opened his eyes, raised his head, squinted at me, and said, "Man, I can't stand Glen Campbell."

"Excuse me, Sir. My father said to tell you we're ready to unload the melons."

One by one, they came off the truck. My brother and I stood inside the big metal box, trying to keep our balance. One of the warehouse workers, Si Lee, stood anchored on the ground. My brother threw the melons to me, I'd catch, then, toss them on. Twenty one, twenty two, twenty three. Big green balls shooting through the universe. Fifty one, fifty two, fifty three. The giant pickles flew off the truck.

When we got bored, we turned the unloading into a game. We threw the melons faster, slower, higher, lower. The object was to be as daring as you could without breaking any. My brother and I always lost our balance and broke a few, but, Si Lee never missed a melon.

Si Lee was pretty old, probably about forty, but, he seemed like a kid because he didn't speak any English. Whatever happened, good or bad, Si Lee just laughed. Before he came to America, he lived on a boat with his family. They were just kind of drifting countryless. My mom hired Si Lee after she read about him in the newspaper. The article called him a "boatperson," but, my mom said he was a Vietnamese refugee. The social worker said he was lucky that he made it to this country. She said there were thousands of people, sitting in boats, with nowhere to go.

We got used to the fact that Si Lee couldn't speak any English, because it always seemed like he knew what we were saying, anyway. Si Lee was like part of our family. When we played hot potato with the watermelons, my dad always found the broken ones, grimaced until his eyebrows touched in the middle, and asked what the hell was going on. Each time, my brother and I stood speechless. Each time, Si Lee would look at the broken melon, then, look back at my father, and say, "Sorry, Mr. Dick."

My father grinned as he watched us work. Huge wax boxes, perched on pallets, lined the gravel driveway. Each box held a hundred watermelons.

"You kids are gonna kill yourselves. Let me get a couple of lumpers. I'll pay 'em twenty bucks and that'll be the end of it."

The Neighbor, hose still in his right hand, beer bottle still in his left, stood listening. He'd been watering his flowers for over an hour and they still weren't wet. One minute, the water was flowing in a steady stream, the next minute, there was barely a dribble.

My older brother stood, his hands gripping the inside of the warehouse door, watching as we worked. "Dad, Cliff Lieu's on the phone. He's over on Laskey near Krogers, the old yellow truck's broke down."

My father peered toward my brother. "What in the fuck you mean the old yellow truck's broke down? What did that son of a bitch do? Doesn't he know they're waiting for those carrots?"

"The truck's broke down."

"Jesus Fucking Christ. Tell him I'll be right there."

13

My father looked inside the truck, shook his head, and pulled at his sagging pants. "Son of a Bitch. Just what I need. The fucking truck's broke down. I just had the fucker fixed. What in the hell am I gonna do about those carrots?"

Si Lee missed a melon. I threw it too high. Instead of falling near his hands, the melon rose like a hot air balloon and fell over his right shoulder.

My father glanced at the smashed melon, then, he looked at me. "Goddamnit to hell. Get off that truck. Didn't I tell you to get off that truck? You kids are gonna kill your fucking selves. Didn't I tell you I'd get a couple of lumpers?"

The melon sat on the ground. Its guts were hanging out. I thought about it riding in the truck all the way from Georgia. I wondered was it true what they said about everything is alive and even the grass has a soul. I thought about how all the melons in the boxes were going to some backyard barbecue or family reunion, and how that one wasn't even gonna make it to Krogers.

"Do you have wax in your ears? Didn't I tell you to get off that truck? C'mon, Goddamnit. I gotta go see about those carrots."

Si Lee stood smiling. He looked at the melon, then, back at my father.

"Sorry, Mr. Dick."

My father looked at Si Lee, shook his head, and walked toward the warehouse. Si Lee hung his head and stared at the gravel. My little brother jumped off the truck, picked up the smashed melon, and carried it to the dumpster.

The Neighbor, holding a beer bottle, but, minus the hose, watched as my father disappeared into darkness. "Hey, pretty boy. Whad I tell ya 'bout those pallets? Huh? Whadda I tell ya? I told ya to quit tippin' that fence. Ya little good for nothin' smartass. You'll get yours, ya little chump change shit."

The Neighbor's face grew redder with each word. My brother changed instantly from a good for nothin' smartass to a hot shit Mr. Pretty Boy. From a worthless piece of shit to a Smartassed Mr. Fancy. The green torpedoes were flying through the air. We had found our rhythm. Seven hundred and twenty. "Lazy assed son of a bitch." Seven hundred and twenty one. "Spoiled rotten golden boy." Seven hundred and twenty two. "Motherfuckin' punk." Seven hundred and twenty three. "Just keep tippin' that fence."

"That guy's a real pain in the ass. How ya'll put up with him? If it'd been me, I'd knocked him on his ass a long time ago." The trucker leaned against a box of melons, rubbed his eye, and lit a cigarette.

"He's harmless, just an old drunk, doesn't even know what he's saying," my little brother shouted while he tossed melons. "We don't have time to fight with him. We gotta get these melons unloaded. Gotta get you back to Cincinnati."

"Harmless or not, somebody givin' me lip like that, I swear, I'd about have to knock him on his ass." The trucker looked at the Neighbor, tossed his cigarette, and kicked at the air in front of him. "Hell, I took two years of karate. Damned near a black belt. Way I see it, I don't take shit from nobody."

"Hey, Rice a Roni," the Neighbor shouted. "What's that you say? Gonna kick my ass? Don't look like no slant eyed foo man chu to me. C'mon, Chop Suey, show me your karate. I ain't a scared a you, China Boy. Kick my ass? Kick my ass? You ain't gonna kick nobody's ass, melon man. You wanna see karate? I'll show you some karate. Look at this, Pony Boy." The old man dropped his beer bottle. His right arm rose, his right leg followed. He stood, a balding bellied ballerina, perched, among pink flowers.

"Look at that jackass," the trucker nodded toward the old man.

My little brother looked at the trucker and tossed another melon. "I told you to ignore him," he said. "We're almost done. Got about a hundred, maybe two hundred more to go. Another half hour and you're outta here."

The trucker kicked at the gravel and lit another cigarette. "Hell, it'd been me, I'd a let those melons rot. No way in hell I'm gonna unload a truckload a melons."

"Hey, you kids want something from Wendy's?" My dad stood at the edge of the truck. The truck was almost empty. He looked inside and grinned. "Your mother and I are going to lunch. We'll be back in about an hour. You sure as shit whipped a job on those melons."

"You got some nice kids here, Mister." The trucker reached into his shirt pocket, pulled out a new pack of cigarettes, tapped the pack with the palm of his hand, and pulled the cellophane. "Hell, I gotta boy won't even take out the garbage. Have to threaten to break his legs to get him to even consider movin.' My old lady and I both work, but, that don't seem to register. He just sits on the couch starin' at the television. Hell, kids these days, they all want somethin' for nothin.' Don't understand you have to work for it. My wife tells him money don't grow on trees, but, he'll just look at her, point at the backyard and say nothin' else does neither. I ever thought about talkin' to my old man that way, that'd be the end of it. He'd a knock'd my ass clear from here to Mississippi. Now, that was one mean son of a bitch. Don't make 'em like that anymore. Hell, you ask me, I'd say this country's gone soft. Think 'bout the great men that built this country. John Wayne and Daniel Boone and all the rest of 'em. Hell, it's a shame. It sure is. Nation like this filled with a bunch of queers and marshmallows."

"Hey, Pretty Boy, didn't I tell you to quit tippin' that fence?" The Neighbor was yelling at his flowers. "Didn't I?" His face twisted and puffed. He picked up the hose, aimed it at the fence, and started spraying.

"Hell, I can't get a word in edgewise." The trucker shook his head and scowled pinch lipped in the old man's direction. "Hey, buddy, why don't ya shut up?"

The old man threw the hose down and ran, with his shoes untied and his big belly bouncing, toward the trailer. "I told ya." Looking like an irritated peacock, he cocked his head, and stumbled, with big white eyes popping, toward the worn blue steps of the trailer.

"That old drunk liked to never leave," the trucker said. "Well, anyway. What I was sayin' was...."

"You worthless piece of shit." The old man stuck his head out of the trailer's bedroom window. "You'll get yours." He pulled his head inside, then, a couple of seconds later, he poked his left arm out. "I warned ya, didn't I?" His elbow twisted right, then left, as the old man clutched a hammer, white knuckle tight, and swung it through the air.

"Hell. He's serious." The trucker looked at my brother. "I'm gonna git in my truck."

"Naaaa. He ain't gonna hurt you," my little brother laughed. "Hell, you

16

some kind of pussy? He's just drunk."

The old man stepped out of the trailer. He stood wobbling on the porch, then he grabbed the rail and eased himself, one step at a time, toward the bottom stair. Once he reached the ground, he waved the hammer, and stumbled, red faced and bleary eyed, toward the break in the fence.

I stopped unloading the melons and watched the old man move. Two hundred pounds of anger inched forward, shook, and popped its neck veins.

"C'mon, Rice a Roni....c'mon." The old man lunged. His right foot caught the hose. He pitched forward, regained his balance, and staggered across the property lines. The trucker grinned, took off his cap, wiped his forehead, looked at my little brother, and said, "I'm outta here."

"C'mon." The old man weaved crookedly toward the trucker. The trucker spit, then ran toward his truck. The old man's eyes darted. "Where's Pretty Boy?" He raised his arm and waved the hammer. "I warned ya. Didn't I?" The hammer danced its metal threat.

"Hey," my father yelled, as he walked toward the old man. He'd been leaning against the warehouse wall, waiting for my mother. "What in the hell's the matter?"

The old man didn't answer. He stopped, glanced at my father sideways, and swung the hammer. My father tried to grab the old man's arm. The hammer swung. Once. Twice. Then, it hit my father's chest. My father winced and fell backward.

"Dad." My older brother stepped from the darkness of the warehouse, dropped a box of lettuce, and ran toward my father.

"C'mon." The old man yelled. "C'mon."

My older brother slid between my father and the hammer. He squinted each time the pointy metal came close to him. I wanted to help, but, when I got scared, I froze. It didn't matter if the house was burning down, or, if there was a tarantula in my bed, when I was afraid, I couldn't move. I stood paralyzed and watched my brother duck and dodge.

The old man sneered as he swung the hammer. He reminded me those metal banks that they sold in interstate souvenir shops. Miniature metal men with beady eyes and pinched faces. Their arms moved up and

17

down each time someone lifted the lever and dropped in a quarter.

The hammer hit my brother's ear.

The old man roared. He'd hit his target.

My brother stumbled forward.

"Goddamnit." My father tried to grab the old man's arm.

People were beginning to gather. Heads bobbed past watermelons. Arms threw fake punches. Feet shuffled toward the fight. A woman, with blonde hair that stuck up like cottoncandy, bumped into me. She lost her balance, grabbed my elbow, steadied herself, and screamed, "Watch out."

The hammer cut the air like a sickle. As soon as it reached the right side, the old man swung it left.

"Hey, grandpa, put your toys away," a bald man shouted. He turned to make sure the crowd was listening, then, he grinned and clasped his hands together. "It's past your naptime, darling."

"Yeah, gramps." A sweaty fat man taunted. "Go home."

The old man's face twisted red. A small string of spit dripped from his mouth, his chest shined wet, his belly hung low, and his shorts were sagging. But, he didn't seem to notice. He swung the hammer, gripped white knuckle tight, at anything that moved.

"Hit the motherfucker," a man wearing sagging jeans and a black t-shirt yelled.

"Two bucks on the kid," a grinning grey man shouted.

"You stupid son of a bitch. Give me that Goddamned hammer." My father tried to catch the old man's arm.

"Make me." The old man sneered.

"Make me my ass," my father shouted. "Put that Goddamned hammer down."

The old man stood breathing heavily. His shoulders were hunched and his shoes were untied. Sweat dripped from the tip of his nose. He glanced at my father and smiled, then he let the hammer fall.

The crowd booed. They wanted to see a fight, but there wasn't going to be a fight. The old man had come to his senses. I knew, as I watched the crowd break up, that the old man could have swung the hammer until his arm fell off, but, my brother wouldn't have hit him.

People were beginning to leave. Some jogged toward the cars they'd left running, parked at the edge of the driveway, like logs jammed in a river. Others lingered. A fat woman, wearing a yellow blouse splattered with black polka dots, flicked her cigarette and watched, slack jawed and squinty eyed, as it flew past a skinny man's head. Once she was sure it hadn't hit anybody and saw the red glowing against the gravel, she turned, looked at the old man, and said, "Ain't that a shame? Man his age acting plum crazy."

"Hell, I can't exactly vouch for grandpa's mental condition," the bald man who'd been shouting earlier said. "But, I'll goddamnedguarantee ya one thing," he spit, then nodded toward my brother, "that's either the bravest son of a bitch on two feet, or, the world's biggest pussy."

Blood covered the top half of my brother's t-shirt. His face was drenched with sweat, and his ear was bleeding. My father shook his head and said, "What a fucking day."

"You've got that right," my brother grinned. "But you know what the real pisser is?"

"What's that," my father asked.

"Looks like you missed lunch."

"Yeah, well, guess I'll have to eat one of those watermelons." My father looked at me and winked, then he put his arm around my brother's neck, turned, and guided him toward the warehouse.

The old man stood staring straight ahead. He hadn't moved since he let the hammer fall. He looked like a cardboard version of himself. Like a blind man waiting to cross the street. I ran as fast as I could toward my father and my brother who were already halfway to the warehouse.

"Hey. Wait a minute." The old man sprang to life. "Wanna talk to ya." He walked toward my father. "Gotta ast ya somethin'."

"Yeah, what's that," my father stopped and asked.

"Well. Gimme a minute. Lemme get there." The old man lumbered along. The hammer dangled at his side. "Gotta tell ya somethin."

My father looked at the old man with suspicion. His head was tilted and his eyebrows were cocked. He reminded me of the way people look when a person that's been missing for years, suddenly shows up and acts like you've been going out together every week for spaghetti.

"Gimme a minute." The old man staggered.

"Okay," my father said, "but, hurry up, I gotta get to work."

The old man made his way. One foot placed slowly in front of the other. "Well." He looked at my father. "Wanna talk to ya." His cheeks puffed. He leaned to the left. He leaned to the right. He straightened, glanced at my father, and spit. "Gimme a minute."

"Okay." My father waited.

"Wanna show ya somethin'." The old man looked toward the street. He staggered, then steadied himself. He stood staring blankly. Without warning, he lunged forward, grabbed my arm, and swung the hammer toward my father's head.

"Daaad," my older brother screamed.

The old man smirked. The hammer arched right, arched left, then hit my brother's neck. The old man stumbled forward, swung again, and clipped my brother's eye. "Whaddi tell ya?" The old man drew back his leg and kicked. His face was red. His nostrils flared. "Didn't I tell ya?" The old man charged. "Didn't I?"

"Kill the motherfucker." The bald man suddenly reappeared.

"Hit him. You fuckin' pansy." An anonymous voice shouted.

My brother flew at the old man. The old man rushed with the hammer, hit him, fell backward, and swung again. My brother grabbed the old man's arm. The old man snorted, kicked, and dropped the hammer.

"Get him." My father shouted. "Kill the sonofabitch."

"Kill him. You fucking faggot." The woman with the polka dotted blouse screamed.

My brother hooked the old man's leg. The old man fell. My brother jumped on top of him.

"Kick his ass," my father yelled.

"Kill him." A fat man shouted.

My brother pressed the old man's face into the gravel. He pounded, punch after punch, and jab after jab, until the old man didn't move. Until the old man didn't struggle. Until his eyes were stuck open. Until silence slivered in like a snake. And the only thing I could see was a tiny red trickle at the edge of the old man's mouth. And the only thing I could hear was my mother saying no and no and no.

Kevin Parry

Joint second in the Fish Short Story Prize

Was born in Umtata, South Africa, and has lived in England since 1979. Educated at various universities in both countries. Formerly worked in retail but now writes full time. Has won a number of prizes, and his story, *The Pie,* was published in *Scrap Magic* – Fish's '98 collection –

Drowned Boy

Kevin Parry

The day I didn't kill myself began like this, too: the dream about the drowned boy again, then waking into this room, this stillness. So still, it's like waking into the drowned boy's dream of me. I open my eyes. The dark floorboards slide from beneath the bed, converge in the black slit under the door like a wedge; the limp torso of my school blazer hangs on the open door of the wardrobe; the wardrobe is full of darkness. I lie here, listen: not a sound. Listen. Within the walls of this house, the shell of this room, the bones of this skull, I am quite, quite alone, a distillation of nothing in the silence of the universe. I close my eyes. I begin to masturbate.

That day was the first time I'd got close to really doing it. I took Dad's revolver from his drawer. The cold dead-weight of its black steel in my hand. So perfectly it fitted my palm, like it had been waiting there just for me. I put the barrel into my mouth, icy against my lips and tongue: the slick taste-smell of gun oil, my teeth fragile on the steel. I watched myself in the mirror, my finger on the trigger, squeezing ever so slightly, and thought about doing it. But the reflection in the mirror was wrong, somehow, not really me; I couldn't quite recognise myself in it. It's something like what I feel with Maureen, I suppose (I don't know her name; I've never spoken to her. I call her Maureen. *Maureen*). I get to school early enough to be up at the classroom window when the Clifton

23

Girls' bus stops below. She gets out with all the others, then looks up at me, shyly, secretively, and smiles. I smile back. But I always have this vision of what I look like from down there. I hate it, the thought of her seeing this white isolated face framed in the window as me. It's a prison, your idea of how other people see you, how you see yourself; you can never escape from it. Maybe that had something to do with why I couldn't really accept that kid in the mirror with the barrel in his mouth as me. I lowered the gun. I'd never fired one before, so, just for interest, to see if it was actually loaded, I pointed it out of the window at the grass bank and pulled the trigger. The report was deafening.

Cole came round that afternoon, I remember – he used to come round, then. I didn't tell him about it. But I showed him one of the clippings I've collected from newspapers, one about this kid, also sixteen, who'd hanged himself. He left a note saying there was no problem, it was just that the idea of death, of dying, excited him, that he just couldn't wait to find out what happened afterwards. Cole couldn't understand it: 'Bloody nutter, Tom,' he said. Not very deep, Cole; doesn't think about things much. He told me once that he had a twin sister who died at birth. I went and found her grave in the city cemetery one afternoon after school, a little grey headstone with her name on it. I could never look at Cole after that without thinking of her in him, how his eyes, his teeth, fingernails, saliva might be identical to hers, how little dead Susan lived in him and part of him was buried there in the cemetery, mingled with her little heap of chicken bones. It's a strange excitement, knowing something so secret about a person, watching them laugh, talk, yawn, and seeing their death real and living in them, like a relentless vine.

What I felt when I saw the picture of the drowned boy, though, was something else. As I turned the page and saw him the recognition was like an explosion inside me, of shock, yet also of excitement; a glow of relief; frightening, yet a sort of bliss. Who he was, I had no idea – but I recognised him instantly. He didn't resemble me, except in the most general way – round face, dark hair, fair complexion – yet my own self, somehow, stared back at me out of his eyes. It was like we remembered each other.

I rode out to Ottery Dam late that afternoon, past the small overgrown quarry and across the horsefield. I go there often now, sometimes twice a week; but that was the first time. There was no one about. I left my bike against the stile, crossed the railway track and walked down the narrow footpath. I could see the dam below: the willows, the dark oval of water. I went down and stood on the concrete retaining wall and looked around. The place was deserted and still. I waited. I used to get photographs of dead people – any person who seemed somehow familiar or attracted me – and find the location of the picture and go and stand in the exact spot where they'd stood, touch the handrail or the step or the tree that they'd been touching, and try to think my way into them, be them, think them back into me. The photo of the drowned boy was just a head-and-shoulders shot against a plain background; I couldn't have used it like that. But I didn't need any photographs at the dam: standing on the wall, waiting, watching the hulking forms of the willows, the earth banks, the still water so dark in the fading light, the feeling filled me like a tide. Down in the water below the wall, my reflection towered up against the slow, darkening clouds. I stripped off my clothes and lowered myself from the wall, naked, into the cold depth of my reflection. As I stroked slowly toward the willows where the water was profoundly black, the pale face, the form, kept perfect rhythm beneath me, and the thick loamy odour of mud rose up from the stirred water like a strange, forgotten, longed-for memory retrieved at last.

I cup the warm little pool of semen in the palm of my hand, grey-white, the origin of things; the ammonic smell of those pools where life's slime began. Fish-eyed on the gleaming surface, is it the reflected silhouette of my head that I can see, framed against the convex window? I let it run off, drip; my sticky palm shines like a mollusc's trail in the dim light. So quickly it cools; cold, clings; phlegm from the drowned boy's lungs.

I stand in my night-dress in the dark passage, my ear to Tom's door. Through my heart's storm I can hear his dream. Yes, this place again: the black water, the silence, the slow tear of his skin – ankles, elbows,

25

cheekbones, knees – as he drifts and drags across the teeth of the concrete: he's at the bottom again. The stagnant water thick as tar; his motions a lethargic agony of slow rolling, pressure bursting his eardrums, lungs imploding. I clamp my hands over my mouth and scream to him in my head, *My boy, you can breathe, you can breathe!* And, at the moment of absolute unendurability, he does remember: he *can* breathe. He opens his mouth and sucks the black metallic water in, gasps down great lead-heavy lungfuls of it, deep as he can – *breathes* it. And so he is released, the water turning thin and lacy as air as he glides up through the sun-shafted shallows toward the golden circle of the surface.

I crumple trembling down onto my haunches in the black still passage, squat in the cold sweat of relief, having birthed again, delivered him again from those dark waters.

My hands are clammy against the cold wall as I feel my way back down the passage.

Douglas stirs as I get back between the icy sheets.

'Sarah – ?' he mumbles from under the slow current of his sedation, reaching out, feeling for me.

'Sssssh, go back to sleep,' I say.

He turns over and I listen to the ebb of his breathing as sleep tides over him again.

I have to be careful with Douglas.

I lie quite still when he gets up in the early morning, my eyes shut tight. He dresses quietly, not wishing to wake me. He leans over me, kisses my cheek lightly. I do not move, keep my breathing low and even. 'My love,' he whispers under his breath, then tiptoes out. I listen to the front door click shut, the car cough and accelerate down the road. I do not stir, wait for the sound to recede, diminish, vanish into the mist of distant crows' calls. Then I get up quickly, quietly; stand in the doorway, listening. The dark throat of the passage swallows me in the house's silence. At the far end the dim rectangle of Tom's door stands blank as a slate stele. I tiptoe down the passage, stop by the door. I wait; listen. Not a sound. Just the rasp of my night-dress as I breathe, furtive and crustacean. Yes, he's still asleep. *My boy: sleep!*

I wait in the lounge, inch the curtains apart with my finger; a little grey light shafts the submarine gloom of the room. Out there, nothing. The long road empty; leaves, limp. Everything still.

Then I see him, the new doctor, walking quietly – stealthily – up the drive. He's parked his car in the road; perhaps to make less noise. I suspect Douglas asked him to call; he wants to rake it all up again. That's why he wanted this new doctor: 'He's a specialist: give him a chance: talk to him: he can help.' I told Douglas: it's rest Tom needs. Not disturbance, questions, upset. Not dredging everything up again, why Tom tried to do it, why, why. We've been through it all before. The whys don't matter now.

I watch him climb the steps. Then I jerk the door open before he can ring the bell. He is startled, stands there shuffling on the mat in his dark suit. 'Oh, I – just thought I'd pop in – ' he says, ' – on my way to the hospital: see how things are.'

'Tom's still asleep,' I say softly. 'I don't really want to wake him.'

'Oh – I see – yes,' he says, eyelids batting.

'The *dream* again last night,' I tell him.

'Ah, the dream – same one again, was it?'

'Yes. The same one.'

He looks over my shoulder into the lounge, perhaps thinking I'll invite him in. But I don't. I say: 'It *is* rest he most needs, *isn't* it?'

'Well, of course,' he says, ' – yes.'

'That's what I keep telling Douglas. Rest.'

'Oh, yes, that's fine – absolutely,' he says.

I don't say anything more then. He shuffles again. Then he says, 'And how about you, Mrs Shone: are you feeling OK?'

'Yes,' I say. 'Of course.'

Again, that rapid little spasm of blinking, like a live wire into my nervous system.

He pauses a moment; then he says, 'Could I come in for a minute, would you mind – have a little chat – ?'

'No, I'd rather not, now,' I say firmly. 'I really don't want Tom disturbed.'

'All right,' he says. 'That's all right, I understand. Well – another time – I'll look in again – '

I watch him until he's half way down the drive. Then I call: 'Did Douglas ask you to come this morning?'

27

'Douglas?' he says, stopping, turning. 'Oh, no, not at all. No, why do you ask?'

I wonder for a moment whether I shouldn't talk to him about Douglas.

'It's nothing,' I say.

He hesitates, then turns and continues down the drive. I close the door quietly and watch him through the curtains. He sits in his car for a minute, writing. Then he drives off, peering up at the house.

She sits across the table, still in her dressing gown, watching me as I eat my supper, her white thin fingers picking, picking at an embroidered flower on the cloth. Her eyes are ringed by bruises, the brown of crushed apples. At night in bed she makes to swallow her sleeping pill with a sip of water; after three weeks the pill-bottle remains full to the brim. I tuck my pills, each night, one by one, into a ball of socks at the back of my drawer. During the night I hear her slip out of bed, inch down the passage to Tom's bedroom. I lift myself up and listen: nothing. The house hollow as a seashell, gushing silence. Nothing: just the thin rasp of blood in my ears. She's out there for twenty minutes, sometimes – thirty, perhaps. I feign sleep when she comes creeping back. Sometimes, though I try to fight it off, exhaustion washes me under and I wake with her slipping quietly back between the sheets. In the morning when I get up for work *she* makes *her* dissemblance of sleep, her white face – so like Tom's, it is – tensely still in the middle of the uncreased pillow. We can't go on like this.

I chew and swallow, chew and swallow, avoid her gaze. My eyes linger around my plate – tablecloth, saltcellar, sideplate, jug – settle at last in the bowl of a spoon. Peering over its opposite edges, the blank ovals of our faces, seen from below, are framed against the distant arena of the ceiling: the room tumbles inwards upon us in a smear of warped angles, curtains, walls, sideboard, shelves, an amphitheatre of impossible perspectives.

A tic in the corner of my consciousness brings her fingers back into focus, still picking, picking away at the cloth, and I realise I have matched my chewing to their rhythm.

I lay my knife and fork down on the plate and look her directly in the eyes. This has to end.

'What did you do today?' I say. Knowing she's been in her dressing gown all day. Sitting around. Waiting.

Her eyes flicker faintly as they focus; but the rhythm of her fingers never falters.

'Some dusting – ' she begins, words already failing her. 'Ironing – things – '

'Did anyone call?' I've chosen the wrong word; her mind flutters for an instant between the ambiguities, escapes through the unintended sense.

'No. No calls.'

I persist, determined to bring it all to a head: 'Did anyone come round, then?'

She does not hesitate: 'No.'

'Didn't the doctor come round this morning?'

'Why? Did *you ask* him to come?'

'I'm asking *you* if he *did* come.'

She remains silent.

'Did he come, Sarah?'

'That doctor – all this again – I'm not discussing it,' she says.

'Christ, Sarah, we *have* to discuss it,' I say. Grasping at her hand to restrain the relentless fingers, I knock the jug off the table. It explodes on the floor.

'Oh, *shuuuush* – !' she cries, jumping up and shutting the door.

I stare at her. 'Why do you close the door – ?'

'Tom's aslee – '

And it's out: the subject, the name, the unmentionable word at the centre of it all, the horror round which, in silence, suspicion, pretence, we circle and circle each other.

'Sarah, listen,' I plead, 'listen, I've asked the doctor to come tomorrow – '

'I won't have it, Douglas. Why *do* you have to keep raking over it? It doesn't *matter* why Tom tried to do it; in the name of God, can't you just leave it alone! All he needs is rest – even that doctor of yours agreed – '

'Sarah, Tom is – for Christ's sake, when are you going to get it into your fucking head? Who do you think it was they fished out of Ottery

29

Dam? Who do you think that drowned boy was? You're just going to have to accept it – '

She jumps up from her chair, snatches the door open, runs on tiptoe down the passage. She comes back, unfolding a crumpled sheet of newspaper, thrusts it under my nose, her hands shaking violently.

'Read it!' she hisses, pushing the door to. 'Who does it say drowned in Ottery Dam? Go on, tell me, who was it? Who?'

I look up from the clipping into her trembling unfamiliar face, her eyes, wide and unrecognisable, wild and round as some bird's.

'Sarah – what are you doing – ?' I say. 'What is this? This clipping: it's one of Tom's, from his drawer, that bloody collection of clippings he made. Look at the date – this is two years old – Tom – '

'I don't care about the date, I told you to read the name. *Read* it! Don't sit there staring at me like that, *read it!*'

But I cannot take my eyes off her face, the terrible alien lagoons of her eyes.

She slams the clipping down on the table in front of me, begins to pummel me with both hands, on my back, my shoulders, my head.

'*Read the fucking name!*' she screams. 'Do I have to spell it out for you? Look *there: there*: does that say "Tom Shone"? *Tell me! Where does it say "Tom Shone"* – ?'

I shield myself from her flailing arms, grip her round the waist as I crouch on my chair, crush her to me, crush my head to her body, the primitive choked sobbing that has taken possession of me seeming to come from somebody else in some other room, some distant life beyond recall: '*How can you leave me like this? Sarah, how can you leave me like this?*'

And under this mantra that racks me, that will not cease but can never be enough, her blows have slowed, have stopped; turned to caresses. Cradling my head to her breast, she strokes my hair, my cheek, whispers, 'Hush, my darling, hush,' rocking me to and fro to the distant rhythm of my sobs. I shut my eyes tight. Darkness, a vacuum through which her hushing lilts and sways like water lapping, and like the dreamy motion of willows on the surface of a pool, her stroking fingers, her impossible words: 'All right. All right. Sssssssh. It's going to be all right. My boy.'

Eleanor Flegg

I was born in Dublin in 1967. I have two children, a Highland pony, a lurcher and a pressing need to earn my living. We lived in Russia and Scotland before returning to live in Ireland in 1998. I write very sporadically because of family and other pressures, but whenever I am on the verge of giving up I get something published and decide to keep going. I won the Hennessy Award in 1995, which kept my spirits up for years! I have written a novel set in the German Reformation. I like this novel a lot, but nobody else does much, so it has not been published and I am trying to write another on a more appealing topic.

The Lobster Shift

Eleanor Flegg

Temptation came to Ferdia in the heat of the day. During the breathless afternoons when he sought sleep under an open window and desire crept up on him like a thief. The craven desire for an all powerful, all seeing God. An ancient longing. As old as the hills.

It was tiredness that had him in this state of mind. Tiredness and a helpless sense of destiny. As though a prophecy had him by the hair.

The vigour drained out of the day. Ferdia slept. Outside his apartment the hot city panted on through the night. Dreams broke the surface of his sleep and gathered like pearls in the cleft of his chin. He drew his damp hands upwards over his face. Rubbed the sweat back into his skin. He was oiled and moist with sleep; his hands smelt of mushrooms. He dreamt of a God who enfolded him like a lover. A God who waited on the brink of disaster with hands outstretched. Poised for the missed step, the crack in the pavement, the sudden plummeting fall.

Ferdia cradled his body in his own arms and rolled sideways into another wave of sleep. The F train pulsed like an artery under the street.

The drug dealers kept him awake at night; their calling like prayer outside his window. China white, china white. A breath of words so soft that it might have been imagined. They were a movement of ghosts on street corners. The used blood draining back through the veins of the city. If he

33

turned towards them, they faded. Faded into doorways, into moving cars. Their movements were barely perceptible. Never, not once, did they look him in the eye. Even when they had gone he could hear their murmur in his ears. China white, china white. It was a mantra. The sound of the sea.

At these times he felt that the Messiah was waiting for him on the street outside, lounging against the corner with the drug dealers. Messiah; a passionate word.

He rang the police.

There are people selling drugs outside my window.

So?

So it's legal?

Coming home in the dark he saw a squad car parked on Curzon Street. The police were snorting coke in the front seat, laughing. At the crossroads, business carried on as usual. Ferdia felt like soft clay between the fingertips of the city.

He lived on Clinton Street over a launderette. His apartment smelt of washing machines and fabric conditioner. The rooms filled up with steam. The scent of fabric under a hot iron. If he pressed his ear to the wall he could hear the pulse of tumble dryers vibrating. Tiny mice, the size of his thumbnail, ran up the walls of the building and came in through the high windows. He threw them out again, having heard that a mouse is too light to hurt itself in a fall. He could not bring himself to kill them.

The window at the back of his apartment looked out over an empty lot. A dumping ground for stolen vehicles. A haven for those with no bed for the night. Once, he saw a man with no arms lifted up into the back of an old truck. His friends tied a stocking around his leg and found the vein. Ferdia was appalled to see that they were sharing needles. He imagined himself standing on the fire escape, showering down armfuls of needles on the empty lot. He saw them glitter like tinsel in the hot, polluted sunset: clean syringes in their plastic wraps, tourniquets, teaspoons and sterile swabs. Rattling through the metal lattice onto the roof of the truck below.

Ferdia walked the streets of the Hispanic quarter. He was feeling his way. The shops on Clinton Street sold dried and tinned produce, all of it labelled in Spanish. The girls behind the counter stared at him as he walked the sparsely stocked aisles. He could see nothing that he wanted to buy. Nothing that would add up to a square meal. Sometimes he was able to select something simple; pasta or rice. Otherwise, not wanting to walk out empty handed, he gathered a basketful of unidentified tins. He had the impression that they were laughing at him. At home he would open the tins with trepidation. Find fruit in syrup or pickles of astonishing bitterness. Ferdia ate them dutifully, absorbing the experience on his tongue.

On St Mark's Place he ate breakfast in a café where it seemed that he was the only one eating alone. He read his book fitfully. No one else was reading. He ate quickly and left. On the street corner a man with a bicycle stopped him.

You want to buy it?

How much?

Forty dollars.

Ferdia tested the bicycle up the one way street. It balanced sweetly beneath him. He felt that he had been given wings. He paid forty dollars and slung his bag around his shoulders. Already he felt integrated.

Ferdia worked the night shift in a restaurant in the meat district. The graveyard shift. The lobster shift. The dark hours when the shellfish were drawn in from the sea. His sleep patterns were all disconnected. Much of the time he felt that he was dreaming. He slept fitfully through the afternoons and woke as the rest of the world was going to bed. Ironed his shirt and pulled on clean black jeans. His bicycle ran like a dream through the dark streets heading West to the rim of the Hudson River. The city fled by on either side of his streamlined body. A flight through the night air. Steam rose from the gratings as though something evil were going on underneath.

He was an incompetent waiter, unskilled and forgetful, with a scant knowledge of the wine list. The other staff bore him up, covering for his mistakes as if he was a beginner. He had been working there for nearly a year. The menu still seemed strange to him: five different types of lettuce, lobster, red snapper and asparagus. Cream soda. The owner kept him on for his Irish accent and his looks. Ferdia's heavy beauty hung over him like a shadow. He felt himself to be as soft as butter. How ripely he would fill the arms of a lover. And still he slept alone.

Twice a week he worked with Eddie, a feral boy from New Mexico. He was a sharp waiter; alert and prompt. They had offered him an evening shift, but Eddie said that it suited him to work nights. In the afternoons he went to the outdoor swimming pool and slept for a few hours, he said that he didn't need much more sleep than that. And Ferdia thought of his own mattress, moulded into the shape of his sleeping form.

The restaurant was something of a high-class diner. The tourist guide described it as terminally hip. Plastic and stainless steel under a pink neon strip light. It was notoriously difficult to find. That was part of the attraction. All through the night, people burst in the door with cries of relief.

We were walking around for hours!

Ferdia himself, heavy with sleep, often got lost on the way. His shift started at two in the morning. He knew that they would never let him work the daylight hours.

The other waiting staff were actors, artists and dancers; their lives split between how they made money and what they really did. Their bodies were lithe and expectant. They moved through the jungle of tables with predatory grace. Ferdia felt the clumsiness of his own body. The softness of flesh around his waist. And the complete absence of ambition in his life.

I wait tables, he said. That's it.

They admired his modesty.

The diners thinned out into the night and people came in from the clubs in trickles. They were sweat-stained and hungry for burgers and fries. Their clothes were made of leather and diving equipment. Sometimes they had dogs with them, pedigree dogs, immaculately trained to lie beneath the tables. Occasionally their tips were large, but Ferdia did not have the knack of drawing generous tips. He struggled to be friendly and came away with a few dollars.

You try too hard, said Nicole. She was blonde and peremptory.

You gotta treat them like shit.

She made over a hundred dollars a night in tips.

Ferdia opened a bottle of wine. He drank steadily until the morning.

The big black chef came out from his metal kitchen and read aloud from Walt Whitman. Nicole stretched like a ballerina against the counter. She had a strip of lace tattooed down her leg from hip to ankle. The poetry embedded itself in Ferdia's tired mind. He was never quite drunk, but far from sober. The alcohol made him even less competent and he helped himself to cheesecake from the dessert trolley.

Don't eat that shit, Nicole said. It makes you fat.

She lived on sea vegetables and steamed brown rice. But Ferdia craved the dreamy sweetness of unsuitable foods. He thought that he was a different breed from these driven creatures.

As the customers were filtering out into the hot night, a woman leant over the counter to put her hand on Ferdia's arm.

Well boy, she said, you don't do it smoothly but you do it with heart.

Her fingers rested on his arm amid a forest of tiny hairs. The underside of his wrist was soft as velvet. He moved away from her. The touch of another person filled him with longing.

When it grew quiet he dozed in the corner between the two restaurant cats, Breakfast and Lunch. They were so fat that they undulated beneath their fur. Ferdia was fascinated and revolted. A third cat, Dinner, had been killed by a meat truck outside the restaurant. They said that he had been the fattest of the lot.

At dawn he left the restaurant and wandered down to the wharf to throw his empty wine bottles into a dumpster at the water's edge. The manager would be in by eight o'clock to count the empties. The sunrise lit up the glass flanks of huge buildings rising up out of the Hudson River. The sudden light hurt his eyes. It was like a postcard. Like the title sequence of a film.

Through the grid work of streets the trucks rolled into the meat district. The truckers began to unload carcasses. The sidewalk glistened with the effluvia of thawing meat. Ferdia, in his soft leather shoes, picked his way over the slippery offal. On either side of the road, huge warehouses gaped their bloodstained doorways like the mouths of carnivorous beasts.

When they had finished unloading, the truckers came in for breakfast. It was like the restaurant had been transplanted into the path of mainstream America. A regular diner serving breakfast to night workers.

Squat men with overalls and chapped hands.

The chef stood at the hot plate and turned pancakes. Ferdia put on fresh coffee; regular and decaf. He made himself espresso so strong that the machine strained to push water through the massed grounds of coffee. The truckers drank coffee at the bar, talked about their families while the chef cooked eggs. They drove off before the rush hour traffic; polystyrene cups wedged into the dashboards of their trucks.

Ferdia drew breath; wiped his hands on his apron. Alcohol and caffeine vied for supremacy in his blood. He wiped the tables and changed the menu in anticipation of the breakfasters. The fierce, dieting, professional classes. Ferdia put on a tape of Vivaldi. The sleepless night weighed heavily on him, and he struggled with the orders of the recently awoken. Office workers, gathering their adrenaline for an aggressive day. Orange or cranberry juice. English muffins. Eggs over easy. They were particular about every detail of the appalling menu. In his dreams the food used to mutate before his eyes. Sausages becoming hash browns. Eggs turning from scrambled to sunny side up. Customers lurked, dissatisfied, behind their newspapers.

And then he left it all behind and floated out into the bright morning with the cash wages of an illegal immigrant in his pocket. He rode out into the stream of traffic before the heat had time to harden over the city. The wheels of his bicycle flowed freely, sweeping the tiredness out from under him. The world spun, brightly painted, at his feet.

He opened the window by the fire escape and lay down to sleep. The light filtered through the black and white chequered curtain. Traffic and laundry filled the room with their noise and their smells. He turned and lay on his belly. Ferdia slept. Like a great, beached sea mammal that was struggling to breathe beneath its own weight. As he slept he could hear his answering machine taking his calls. He heard his own voice and the tones of electronic music.

When he woke, he played back his messages.

Ferdia, hi! This is Eddie from work. I've been given the night off, do you want to do something? Call me back and leave a message.

Ferdia dialled. The stylised lilt of Eddie's voice seemed to hold infinite possibilities within it. Eddie, whose skin fitted him as loosely as a Labrador puppy's. Whose limbs were joined with rubber bands. He could fold himself into a dozen comfortable shapes. Muscles rippled under his skin.

Eddie drank a glass of orange juice from the fridge and wandered around the apartment. He read the titles of the books on the shelves.

And he reached up and ran his hand down Ferdia's cheek. Hard jaw bone under skin and flesh. The past days had relaxed the bounds of normality and it seemed to Ferdia that all the rules were gone.

Eddie put his hand over Ferdia's.

Hey, babe, let's go down to Clinton street.

In Eddie's company, the drug dealers took on shape and form. He knew their names, and they did not fade from his presence. Ferdia felt that it was he who had become shadowy. The transaction in the doorway was as graceful as a movement in a dance. Eddie barely paused in his walk. And then he turned to Ferdia and kissed his face. A lingering and public kiss. They crossed Houston; surfed up Avenue B on a wave of excitement. The city was a film set; all yellow cabs and mad people at the street corners. Wild Art-gardens built of junk and broken toys. Ferdia felt giddy with anticipation and desire. And with the feeling of normality lying in shreds around him.

Eddie lived in a tiny apartment on 1st Street. There was no window. He took the mirror from above the sink and laid it flat on the table. The ritual of mirror and razor blade and twenty dollar bill seemed like cinema to Ferdia. He could see the childish bulge of his own cheeks reflected in the mirror below him. China white.

He had imagined, for all the damage it might do, a hard toothed drug, but instead it took him in its hands and rocked him gently. Cradled him in the centre of the world. Even as he moved out into the city, Ferdia felt foetal. Embraced.

Eddie and Ferdia walked the dreaming streets. The hard edge had gone from the day. The stars above them wheeled and flashed like a cabaret show in bad taste. As though somebody up there was having a big joke. They walked uptown and climbed the fence into the outdoor swimming pool on Avenue D. The water was as warm as amniotic fluid.

Above the chlorine he could smell the sweat and breath of Eddie treading water beside him. Ferdia felt a surge of freedom rising through him. He felt that he could make love to himself. In his floating arms, Eddie was the strong rubber of gymnasium equipment.

They kissed and floated together. Let the water pull them apart. Flirted with their hunger for each other. Swam closer.

I am way out of my depth, thought Ferdia. And the lightness fell from him as he pulled himself out of the water. He dressed by the side of the pool. On the street corner opposite a group of boys had parked their ghetto blaster and were standing against the wall, not talking. The music was loud, and black, and very fine. In their stillness they had a fluidity that Ferdia coveted. An inbuilt freedom of movement; like the flow of oil.

Yes, he thought, that's what I'm after.

And it seemed to him that the Messiah was back there on the corner in homeboy trainers and a black skin.

Ferdia was constipated for a week. When he looked in the mirror his reflection stared back at him like a stranger. It took him several seconds to recognise himself. His muscles ached as if he was recovering from a fever and he thought that the drug must have split his soul in two.

If Eddie stayed over at the apartment he would wake Ferdia in the night and take him in his arms.

You were crying in your sleep.

But Eddie's hands had no power of healing. While Ferdia slept, his own face was something that was far away from him and that he could not reach. He was at the mercy of nightmares and the strange chemistry of the drug. He thought that it must have driven a crack into his unconscious through which all sorts of unwanted feelings and memories were flooding.

The next time he looked out over the empty lot, the truck had been burnt out. Nobody had seen the fire. It had happened at night, when Ferdia worked and most people slept. He feared for the man with no arms. Were his friends still looking after him? Was there a safe place for them to find a vein in his knotted legs, now that the truck had gone? The lot was deserted; a new set of police padlocks on the gate and the burnt out husks of three cars.

He sensed that Eddie was growing impatient with him. Their lovemaking was something hard and brittle; the branches of trees clashing in a high wind. In these moments of intimacy he mapped Eddie's body with his fingertips; like a chart that might lead him out of himself. A spider tattooed on the muscle of his calf; a lizard on his shoulder blade. These patterns assumed the significance of totems.

In August Eddie went home to New Mexico. He sublet his apartment and was gone. They went down to the dealer on Clinton Street the night before he left. It was not clear how long he would be away. Ferdia ached with the anticipation of loneliness. This was the flip side of the freedom that they had experienced together.

This is my goodbye present, said Eddie. A bag of white powder, one inch square.

They lay out on the fire escape and looked up into the night. It was a Chinese holiday and the Lower East Side was popping with firecrackers. It sounded like gunfire.

Ferdia buried his face in the pillow. He knew that he was due for another week of headaches and constipation. And that the crack that led down into his innermost self had been irreparably widened. Now there was no barrier between him and the things that he didn't want to look at. He was falling off the edge of sanity with his whole life whistling by his ears. Despair overtook him. Sleep no longer seemed safe. He was apprehensive about the horrors that waited for him, and petrified by the lonely tramp across the no man's land between waking and oblivion. Where daytime fears blended into dreams and he seemed to be always on the verge of remembering something so terrible that it shot him into a state of panicked alertness. And so he lay, exhausted and unsleeping, while bad memories tormented him.

The fan stirred the thick air around and around the apartment, like a wooden spoon in a porridge pot. Ferdia sat on the bed and rested his cheek against the cool plaster of the wall. Sweat congealed beneath the surface of his skin, unable to break the surface. Thunderclouds were gathering in the congested sky.

He heard the sound of rain on the fire escape. Heavy drops fast behind each other. A gush; the sky had broken. Locking the door behind him, he walked barefoot up the four flights of stairs onto the flat roof. He stood in the rain. Drenched within seconds, Ferdia peeled off his shirt and stretched his arms up to the heavens. Rivulets of water parted the thick hair on his legs and chest. The drops drummed on his closed eyelids.

And then he was praying. Praying to anyone or anything that he could bring to mind. He reached out his arms unspeakingly to the possibility of God.

Messiah. Christ.

And peace leapt out at him like a mugger from a dark alley, caught and held him in invisible, wrestling arms. He found himself kissed with a violence that took him far beyond pain. That drew him back into himself. That bruised his mouth and quieted his rampaging heart. A tingling flash of light ran through him.

He covered his face in his hands and wept; the palms of his hands smelt of the sweat of God.

A shaft of lightning split the sky and lit the rooftops all along the block. On the opposite side of the street five girls emerged on to the rooftop. They looked around, giggling and talking above the noise of the rain, and slipped off their clothes. Naked, they began to dance on the wet roof. The water flung up splashes around their ankles. Ferdia could see the movement of flesh set free from the confines of clothing; the redness of heat rash underneath their breasts and the marks that tight elastic had made on their bodies. Their wet hair coated their shoulders like silk. The street lay like a gulf between them and the thunder rolled, a great laugh bellowing across the Lower East Side. Ferdia pulled off his sodden shorts and felt the rain flow down his body. The tar beneath his feet was still sticky from the heat of the day.

Although he has lived on the prairies of the American Midwest for more than a decade, Robert Grindy still roams the hills of his native Northern California through his fiction. "Little Stevie" is a selection from his unpublished novel-in-stories, "Feather River Nights," which follows these same characters into adulthood. Grindy teaches writing and literature in Decatur, Illinois ("Soybean Capital of the World"), where he lives with his wife and two children.

Little Stevie Augers In

Robert Grindy

Me and Harp and Dugan looked around for cops then pulled out our Coors and popped them open. "Here's to you, Stevie, you stupid little shit," Harp said. We chugged the beers and stomped down the cans right on the spot where Little Stevie augered in and left them sit there.

We cut seventh period shop to come on downtown and get a good look at the sidewalk under the balcony of the Black Bart Inn. Stevie's parents didn't have a funeral or anything, so this was it. Dugan thought Stevie's folks were probably too embarrassed. I don't think it works that way. Even if your kid *was* killed in a spitting contest, you'd still have a funeral if you had a notion. The guy's dead—who's going to laugh?

Just us. We stood there looking at that balcony then at the sidewalk scrubbed clean except for our cans then at the balcony and just cracked up.

Stevie was a funny little guy with chopped up blond hair and a big mouth full of chew. He was always goofing about something. On the football team he'd be playing defensive back and some big old lineman like me or Harp would come storming out after him and Stevie would whoop and laugh and run in circles. Then if the coach was the quarterback in a drill Stevie would come up and nail him, pads or not. At a rally he got up in front of the whole school and sang "Thank God I'm a Country Boy" all the way through.

Stevie didn't think much about classes, though, so halfway through

45

our senior year they shipped him off to Continuation School so he had half a chance of graduating. And by god he did. Too bad it was the death of him.

They had a ceremony for the seven or eight C-school grads in the upstairs banquet room of the Black Bart. Somehow Stevie managed to get drunk. Even with all his parents and teachers there. Dan Moretti challenged him to a spitting contest out the window. Little Stevie figures that the way to really get distance on a loogy is to take a run at it, get some momentum. So he ran across the room, and just as he arched out a big wet one, he hit the railing, flipped over it and landed on his head on the sidewalk. Broke his neck. Dead before anyone could get downstairs.

We stood there trying not to laugh too much, staring down at the spot where Little Stevie augered in—that's Dugan's line, "augered in." He says it's what fighter pilots call it when they crash. His dad was in Vietnam, and Dugan reads all those *Soldier of Fortune* magazines, so I guess he'd know. That's when I noticed that the sidewalk right there had a funny patch in it—shaped like a heart. It was real old, but you could tell by the color it wasn't the original cement. "What the hell is that?"

Dugan knew. Of course he knew. Anything weird he knew. "That's where the whorehouse plaque used to be." He told us that twenty years ago his uncle and a bunch of Clampers put in a plaque about the whorehouses, just like the other tourist plaques up and down the sidewalk for the hanging tree and the courthouse and crap like that. We're a little quaint-as-hell tourist town in the Mother Lode selling 49er gold rush junk to anyone stupid enough to slow down on the highway. "This plaque was shaped like a heart," Dugan said, "and had a big old hard-on on it so the city council made them take it out. Big old stink about the whole thing."

Of course we thought he was bullshitting us, so he got all excited about how there used to be whorehouses all over Aurora, not just in the 49er days but like back in the 1950s, and open gambling, too. "John Wayne lost $5,000 in a poker game right there in the Black Bart! All those houses on Eureka with the six different outside doors, those were all whorehouses! The mayor was paid off, the police didn't care, then they cleaned them out, so Uncle Guy and Robello's dad and Jack Dummermuth put in this plaque..."

He wouldn't hear nothing until we went upstairs over the Fan Club to his uncle's law office. His secretary was out, so we just barged on in. Guy was stretched out on a couch with the Sporting Green. "Whatta you peckerwoods doing here," he said, "can't you see I'm working."

Dugan got him to tell us all about it. Turns out Aurora was wide open with gambling and whorehouses until the fifties when Pat Brown got elected Attorney General and came in and cleaned the place out. About ten years later Guy and his buddies from E Clampus Vitus, this drinking club that dresses up in 49er gear and pretends to be like the Lions Club or Rotary, they came up with the plaque. They put it in themselves in the middle of the night. Everyone thought it was funny, then some church got into it. "Wasn't even an Aurora church—those holy rollers out in Holyoke." Me and Dugan looked at Harp and started laughing. Guy figured it out. "You one of those Holyoke Washburns? Get the hell out of my office..." but he was laughing too. "TV stations, newspapers, hell all over the country they came in. City council actually approved it. Then we started getting death threats. So we yanked it out one night."

"And no one's seen it since!" Dugan said. "The great plaque mystery!"

"Oh bullshit," Guy said. "It's right here." He moved some cardboard file boxes under an old table in the corner and pulled the plaque off a pile of papers. "I was using it to get the curl out of some old documents. Forgot about it." It was bronze, heart-shaped, about as big as a chocolate box but only about a half-inch thick. It didn't have a boner on it, but it did say "EUREKA STREET BORDELLOS" across the top and "E.R.E.C.T.I.O.N.S." across the bottom. The rest of it said, "The Environmental Resources Enabling Committee To Investigate Our Natural Services herewith pays tribute to those most perfect examples of free enterprise which flourished in this neighborhood for 100 years until consigned to history by political hypocrisy."

That's how we got the idea we should go to a whorehouse. We asked Guy all about the Aurora houses and he seemed to know a lot and after we left we just got to talking about how great it would be if you could just walk into some place and get laid just like that and Dugan—of course it was Dugan—said "Well hell you *can*, up in Nevada they're all over the place," and I think it was Harp who said, "Let's go. Now. Tonight." Next thing I know we're cleaning out cash machines and zipping up the mountain in my car.

Harp was the only one really excited about doing this, but me and Dugan were too stupid and too scared to say no. I know for a fact Dugan had never even touched a girl before—he hardly even went to dances. Though I've never seen anyone more desperate, he's always talking about sex and has a huge pile of porno. I've seen him at beer parties latching on to some girl and just following her around like a puppy when it's so obvious she's trying to lose him. He's a weird looking guy with kind of pointy eyebrows and buzzed hair like his dad. "Shows discipline," he tells us when we kid him about his hair, kind of spitting it out like Daffy Duck. He's skinny and has scoliosis so he stands kind of crooked and can't play sports. Besides all that he's got a bent sense of humor and he's way into guns—not hunting, I don't think he hunts, but big old handguns and assault weapons and all that survivalist crap—so all the girls think he's gross and whacked out, which he is. But when it comes down to it he's shit scared of girls and I'm sure he doesn't want some whore laughing at him the first time he gets anything. And I know I don't. But I can't tell Harp I'm not losing my virginity to some scary old pro. Harp is almost as obsessed with getting laid as Dugan but just not as noisy about it. Hard to get three words out of him, but he does claim he's been getting it regular from Terri Winkler since the eighth grade. I'm not sure about the regular part, but I think he's experienced.

First we were going to head for the Mustang Ranch outside of Reno, but Dugan said that place was just a skanky sex mall for fat truckers off the interstate and where we really should go is this smaller place near Fallon on Highway 50 where all the fighter jocks from the naval air station go. How the hell he knew this I didn't want to know, but that's where we headed, Dugan babbling the whole time like he was the expert—"Don't kiss them on the lips, they hate being kissed, too many diseases and crap..." running on and on—til we got there. Then he was real quiet.

It was easy enough to find—not many buildings along there surrounded by chain-link and barbed wire. A brown boxy building with a bunch of trailers attached to the back. We pulled into the parking lot and Harp said, "All righty then, let's go you pussies." He didn't bother looking at Dugan. Just me. Then he was out the door and inside.

Dugan and me just sat there. This was too weird. Maybe because it was daylight still—like going to a movie, it's supposed to be dark—and we're just off a busy highway and it's just dirty sage and sand and gravel and barbed wire...What the hell is sexy about all that?

Goddamn that Harp Washburn. He really had me this time. If I didn't go in, he would know. If I did go in, he would know. Did I mention he had a sister?

I don't know who moved first but we weren't going to leave the other sit there so me and Dugan went in. It was dark and smelled like stale cigarette smoke. A couple of cowboys were playing pool. A couple more sat at the bar next to women with lots of hair and not so much clothes. Not a guy in the place you'd ever mistake for a fighter jock. I thought I saw Harp across the room at a table with some woman. We sat at the bar quickly so we weren't just standing there looking dumb. Waylon Jennings on the jukebox very loud. Could've been any bar in Aurora except that before we got settled this kind of worn-out brown-haired woman with lots of make-up and a cigarette and big old brown boobs hanging out of a real loose halter top came up and said, "Which one of you boys is going to buy me a beer?" We both started digging out our wallets.

Now in our big plans there were a couple of things we hadn't thought of, the biggest one being that only Harp was even eighteen and you're supposed to be twenty-one, at least to drink, which I thought they wouldn't really care about, but I guess you got to at least look close, and the thing is Dugan looks like he's about twelve, he's so scrawny. The bartender came down. He was a skinny guy with acne scars and a greasy ponytail. He took one look at Dugan and started laughing. "Hey sonny boy, I think we better take a look at your ID," he said. So Dugan gives him his ID and the guy starts laughing even more and shows it to the whore and she starts laughing and Dugan grabs it from her and I grabbed it from him – the worst looking fake ID I've ever seen. You can see how he cut and pasted a picture on top of another ID, "Chuck Quarton," his dad. The thing said he was like forty-seven years old. He was out the door. First time I've ever seen Dugan speechless.

So the guy says to me, "How about you, ace? Let me guess, you're going on fifty-four..." and I'm out of there because I didn't have even a bad fake ID. I'm barely back to the car arguing with Dugan, "I didn't think they'd really look, and I usually just keep my thumb on it..." and out the door comes Harp, the bartender trying to kick him in the ass, you could hear a lot of laughing inside. Now I know Harp has a pretty good fake ID and he looks like he could be twenty-one easy. He was really mad, scary mad. "So, what?" I asked him.

"Fuck off, you shitheads screwed up everything..." and we went at it burning down the highway for about fifteen miles.

Harp calmed down by the time we got to the Highway 88 intersection but he was still pissed off royal. He pulled into a Shortstop and bought two six-packs. "See? It's a good ID, no reason I should've got thrown out if it weren't for you two numbnuts."

We were sitting there in the parking lot drinking beer when Dugan saw the billboard. "Steve Martin! Holy shit!" The sign said he was playing Harrah's Tahoe this month. Thing is Dugan is a big-time Steve Martin groupie. He has all the albums memorized. He did his whole "Let's Get Small" routine at the talent show and tried to do it at the prom (he went by himself) but nobody wanted to hear "die you gravy sucking pigs" and they kicked him off the stage. It was still early and we've got cash burning a hole in our pocket and you don't have to be 21 for a dinner show, so we're on our way.

You *are* supposed to have a jacket and tie though. The maitre'd was a prick, but one of the waiters, a young guy playing with this little moustache, he took pity on us and helped us in the loaner closet and got us a decent enough table, way over on the side but up close. He told us Steve came right down into the audience in our aisle.

We all got prime rib. Dugan wanted his rare and it was still kicking, even he couldn't eat it. Steve Martin was great, even if we were looking at him sideways through the whole thing. He had some new stuff, so Dugan couldn't talk along with him through the whole thing. He had his banjo, his arrows through the head, his wet-mike shocking him. And just like the guy said, he came down off the stage right next to us. He stopped right at the table across the aisle from us with the spotlight on him spilling over onto us. His back was to us and he touched this guy's sleeve, "You know how

50

many polyesters they had to kill to make this suit?" He was so close you could reach out and pinch his ass. So Dugan did.

That made two places we got kicked out of in one night and now both me and Harp were pissed—that was about a twenty-dollar ticket Dugan just blew for us. Even the friendly waiter wouldn't help us. "Crawl back under whatever Deliverance rock you came from, you fucking no class yahoos..." he said. "I don't know, I just thought Steve would think it was funny," Dugan said as we kicked his sorry butt all way back to the car.

I drove us back over the pass, heading on home. Harp and Dugan kept on drinking but I'd had enough. Enough of the whole night. Harp sat there getting quieter and quieter—you wouldn't think a rock could get quieter, but it just sinks into itself. And Dugan just kept running off at the mouth about kicking this bartender's ass and showing that sumbitch waiter what for. "I'd like to see that fairy-ass peckerwood mater-dee when I shove this baby up his butt..." he said. I looked in the rear-view and by the light of the dashboard I could see him in the backseat waving around something dark—goddamn it was a gun.

"What the fuck are you doing!" I screamed and even Harp woke up.

"What what?" Dugan said, scared now, probably because I was swerving all over the road. He didn't seem to get that a drunk kid with a gun in a dark car was the real scary thing in this scene.

We were just passing the turnout to Shot Rock Vista so I hit the brakes and swerved on in there, down a little drive behind the boulders. I jumped out with the car still running and Harp jumped out and fell on his face cussing up a storm and Dugan jumped out with that damn gun in his hand.

"Put it down!" I yelled at him, crouching by the car. "Just put the fucking thing down before you kill us all!"

Dugan was still confused and Harp was no help, he was yelling about never again taking no numbnut jerkoffs out to get laid, but finally Dugan figured out that it was the thing in his hand I was worried about and set it on the roof of the car.

"For christsakes relax, you scared the shit out of me," Dugan said.

First I was going to kill him. Then I'd explain. "Just tell me it wasn't loaded."

"Well of course it's loaded, what the hell's the point of carrying a gun if it ain't loaded, might as well carry a knife with no blade or a pot you can't pee in..."

"A gun?" Harp said. He was interested now and pulled himself up to the car to look.

"Why the hell you got a loaded gun?" I said. "Where was it?"

"In my hip holster, right here." He lifted his shirt up in back. "You think I'm going to a skanky whorehouse without protection?" "A goddamn condom in your wallet would do it, idiot! Someone even *sees* that thing they're gonna shit and next thing you know..."

"I know what the hell I'm doing, I'd never take it out unless. . ."

"Unless you got real drunk and we're driving down the highway. . ."

"Lemme see," Harp said and picked up the gun off the roof of the car.

"Don't let him touch that..." I said, but Dugan was going on about small-weapons codes and hardly noticed Harp holding it.

"This the safety?" Harp said as he pointed it at a car's taillights coming down the highway already past the turn-off.

I heard about three sounds at once and it took a while for each to register in my ringing ears but each was worse than the one before. One was real close and smelly—the bang of Dugan's gun going off in Harp's hand. The other was far away—breaking glass out on the highway. The third was the squeal of brakes out by the breaking glass.

From where we were around the curve of the turnout we could see red taillights getting all wobbly and sideways as the car slid to a stop. The taillights paused a second or two then burned down the highway crazy to get out of there.

"You hit that fucking car, you hit that fucking car," Dugan was almost crying and started banging his head on the roof of the car. Harp was shaking staring down the highway, the gun still sticking straight out in front of him. Then he dropped it and started running drunk circles around the parking lot like he was looking for a rock to hide under. I started chasing him, scared out of my brains, more mad crazy than I'd ever been. I grabbed Harp by the shirt but slipped in gravel and he got away and was in the driver's side with the door locked before I could get it open. Dugan grabbed the gun from the road and fell into the back seat, and Harp threw it in gear with me still hanging onto the handle. Then he slammed on the brakes and I ran around to the other side and just got in before Harp was tearing off down the highway in my car.

Dugan was curled up in the back seat moaning and crying and I'm yelling at Harp to pull over so I could drive and he just kept roaring down the road, and we're way up above the new part so this is thirty-mile-an-hour curves down hill around big old sugar pines and drop-offs a thousand feet into the canyon. We flew past Cook's Station and I looked behind us and saw a car parked crazy next to the pay phone under a utility light in the corner of the empty parking lot. Didn't look like his car had a back windshield, but at least the guy was alive and standing, not holding a bloody head or anything.

I was trying to tell that to Harp to get him to slow down but he just looked in the rearview and missed an easy curve and he slammed on the brake and we slid sideways down the bank into a shallow gully.

When the dust settled we were all okay. Dugan was on the floor in the back moaning even more. I knocked my head on the side window but no blood. Harp had a death grip with locked arms on the steering wheel. We got out and left Dugan crying in the car.

We climbed up the bank on to the road. It was real quiet except for Dugan and very dark except for our headlights in the gully. Harp looked at me. Not like he was sorry or nothing. I don't think he knows how to be sorry. More like, "All right, that's done, let's get to the next thing." We could hear sirens coming up the mountain. The guy at the payphone. Highway patrol. We had maybe five minutes. We stared each other down. Finally I said, "All right. But you owe me. Bigtime. And you know what it'll be." Maybe I didn't say that. Maybe I just thought it. I didn't need to say anything. Harp knew. Did I mention he had a sister?

Harp slid down the bank to the car. He came back with Dugan's gun. I went down the highway to flag the CHP. I could hear Harp shoot out the back window of my car.

By the time we got towed out of there, got the little glass cuts on Dugan patched up, and gave the whole story to the CHP and three sheriff deputies, it was two in the morning before we got back to town. I did most of the talking and the CHP seemed to buy it. I think it helped a lot that

Dugan was screaming so loud and had some cuts. I told them we were just passing Shot Rock Vista when we got hit and I got so scared I finally lost control of the car. We had to fess up to the drinking because of the beer cans and the smell, but I was okay legally to drive. I think it made our story better that we would give them that—hey, we're no angels, sure, just some poor slobs out having a good time when some highway sniper shoots us up, just like that poor fella back up at Cook's Station. Harp was smart enough to bury both the gun and Dugan's holster under a big rock. It worries me how his mind works, how he can be so stupid then figure out this kind of crap so good. He told Dugan we could come back and get it later.

We'd had a lot of rides between us, me and Harp. Usually the rider owed. Tonight Harp drove and he went way over the line, so far over there was no going back. Now I had him. Now I had him. A long time I'd been scraping around after him. He'd had me in his pocket. Thamara. We never talked about it, but we both knew we knew. Thamara. Did I mention he had a sister?

When we finally got back to Harp's house—we dropped off Dugan, still snivelling, at his place—when we finally got to Harp's house—I had to call my parents and tell them I was okay, not that they believed me—when we finally got back to Harp's house it was dead of morning and I was so dead tired but still so tight wired that I hardly knew up from down, but by then my mind had narrowed down to just one thing, like a camera shutter stopping down—Thamara.

She was the only reason I hung out with that prick Harp Washburn. She was the only reason I'd waste hours watching football at his house or putting around his ranch on some stupid little dirtbike. Harp knew that. He never said anything, but when she came into the room or out into the yard he'd stare at me and smirk or chase her off and laugh at me. I knew I was obvious, but I couldn't help it. She was just fifteen, almost one thing not quite another. Pretty. Scary pretty. Long blond hair. Thick eyebrows. Dark eyes. Tall. Legs you never saw, just calves and ankles and little white feet sticking out under long skirts or barefoot at the end of blue jeans. Didn't smile much. She wasn't like sexy or anything—in fact she went way out of her way not to be—but something about the way she'd stand inside those baggy clothes or those prissy church dresses—there was a body in there, all right, and god only knows what it was doing. Something about that long hair, all tied into a thick rope at school but flopping around messy at home, something about the way she chattered on so full of herself and righteous without even hearing herself. Sometimes it seemed like she was standing outside of herself watching, like she started a wind-up toy and stood back watching it go. She'd chatter on about her church group not even looking my way but the whole time I felt like she was circling around and around. The more I hung out there the closer those circles got till I could feel her breathing down my neck and brushing up against me. Never occurred to me to ask her out or make a move or anything. But I never knew I could be so full of some kind of *want*, some kind of want I couldn't even put my finger on it.

I followed Harp in through the garage door. He hadn't bothered calling his parents and they didn't wait up. They had given up on him, I knew that already. I followed him down the back hall. Goddamn that Harp Washburn had played me like a fool long enough and now goddamn it he'd play *my* tune, and the *want* to step on his head once and for all and the *want* for Thamara were so mixed up I stepped inside her bedroom door as Harp held it open.

Harp shut the door and the click shut me down. It was dark and quiet. Just the breathing of Thamara and her sisters, two or three younger ones, I couldn't remember. I had no idea who was anywhere.

Goddamn Harp Washburn. God*damn* Harp Washburn. He did me again. What the hell did I think I was going to do here? Nothing. I figured it out just that second. He figured it out three hours ago. Not that he wouldn't pimp his sister if he could, the asshole. Just wouldn't need to. But here I am standing hot and bothered in a kids' room in the middle of the night, their parents sleeping two doors down. I'm the one in a shitload of trouble again. And Harp's in the bathroom having himself a good long piss.

My eyes adjusted to the dark enough to see I was standing next to Thamara's bed. I could see a thin sheet loose around her. I could see her bare arms stretched above her head. I could see her hair wispy around her forehead. Her eyes were open. She was watching me. How long I don't know.

For the first time that night I was really spooked. I felt like I was coming undone. I started to shake. My fingertips. My kneecaps. My chin. She looked like she had been awake for hours. She didn't look scared, or confused, or curious. Not quite like she was expecting me, but not like she was surprised either. There I was. She wasn't going to say a word, not now, not ever. But she could.

Now Thamara had me. Harp had handed me off. A rush spun through me from my quivering toes to my dizzy head. It was my life, rushing past and ahead too fast to see but sure in its direction.

I'm going to blame it all on Little Stevie.

Sami Moukaddem

Born in Lebanon in 1967, of Brazilian-Lebanese extraction, Sami has been living in Ireland for the past fifteen years. An accomplished musician, by day a counselling psychologist working with adults sexually abused in childhood, at night Sami is locked in the basement by his loving wife who insists he produces great literary works. So far, this discipline has produced seven novels and two collections of short stories. With the birth of his daughter, Princess Samira, Sami has been inspired to unleash his work upon the world. "Ahmad's Teeth" is the first of his works to be published.

Sami can be reached at: sami@iol.ie

Ahmad's Teeth

Sami Moukaddem

Among all the buildings on this street I'm the tallest one. Seven floors high, four apartments to each floor, and a balcony for each apartment. The apartments in my back face taller buildings than I, most of them about eight floors high but none higher than that. The view from my front was better when I was first put up, but that was a long time ago.

Now it's Lebanon in July 1976 and the Civil War doesn't make anybody proud. I'm old, looking my age, but with no bullet holes. The troubles haven't come this way, and I hope to God that they don't, and this is the reason why Ahmad and his older brother Habib have come to stay with their aunt. Anyway...things get confusing with this war and it's difficult to think, even for a building, but anyway, they're on the sixth floor now, since yesterday.

Ahmad is five and a half, Habib seven, and their mother has died from a bad disease. Their father is fighting with some militia and he's been captured by another militia. Their aunt had to collect them after their mother died. She died about six months ago and their father wanted to keep them around for as long as possible, letting the neighbours mind them every now and then, but now he's captured, so this aunt had to take them.

Their aunt is a really nice person, in that she means well, but she's fat. Fat is not that bad but Ahmad's mother wasn't fat. She was slim, had an easier temperament, and she used to brush Ahmad's hair really gently.

She annoyed him sometimes but not in a nasty way, she would want him to brush his teeth before he went to bed and first thing in the morning. He didn't mind brushing at night although he didn't like it too much, but the mornings? No, it didn't make too much sense because he wouldn't have eaten anything all night. His mother would say "Just in case you have eaten something in your dreams", and then he would try to make some sort of a deal with her, that he will brush only on the mornings when he had eaten something in his dreams and then, while doing something else at the same time, she would say "What if you had dreamt and forgotten", and he would be all attentive trying to answer her but in the end he knew that his mother wanted him to brush his teeth. Last night, after their aunt cooked them their meal, she said to both of them not to forget to brush their teeth when they are supposed to. Ahmad already feels that there is something missing.

For the past two months now Ahmad and Habib have made some friends with the neighbours though the aunt is a little bit overprotective. She tells them that she has to be extra careful because they are her responsibility. 'Responsibility' means that they're not really her kids and she can't do whatever she wants with them and if they hurt themselves very badly then she would hear a lot of blame from their father. "But we'll tell him it was our fault". She wants to be easier, more relaxed, and she feels for them, but she still can't do it. She lets them out, but they have to be in her sight; if she comes out to the balcony she wants to be able to see them, and if she can't see them then they should be within hearing distance to respond to her. They play, but not like the other kids who can go a bit further to the next two streets.

Their aunt is also a little bit smelly sometimes. The days get hot and she would have been knitting and she would have had a shower the previous day and she would want to have another one but she couldn't be bothered – these are just some of the habits that come from living on her own. Ahmad's mother was never smelly, she also never put on perfume like the other people who would come and visit her, well, she would only put it on then, but for the rest of the time she didn't need to. She had her own smell; soft, really nice, and it was her, nobody else smelled like that.

He would get glimpses of it every night when she gave him a few kisses before she left him to sleep, but he got the full scent when he cried. She would hold him against her chest, and by the end of his crying he would be waking up to her scent, and then she would say something to him that would allow him to tell himself that he could stop crying now, that if he wanted more of her touch and smell he could always cry later. Well, it might be difficult to just invent something to cry about but if he really wanted to, he knew he could, so he would stop, and he would start to miss her smell as she withdrew from him, but then very quickly she would distract him by coming up with something for him to do, something that he would him lose himself in.

I can hear Ahmad thinking, "Now there is less to do", even though where he used to live there weren't that many kids around. On some days he would go over to his mother and he would hang out of one of her sleeves, "I'm bored...I'm bored...I'm bored...I'm bored...I'm bored...", and he would get to enjoy his mother's huffing. She would huff but not lose her temper even though he would be going on and on, and he knew he was going on and on, and he would enjoy it, and no matter what she said it was going to be a "no, I don't feel like doing that", and every now and then she would come up with something that he *would* like to do but he would keep it to himself and do it later after he had finished with her, or after she really begged him, and he didn't want her to be *really* huffing because then she would start spilling things and she would get mad with herself and he didn't want that to happen to her.

With his aunt it's different. If he tells his aunt that he is bored, it would end up being up to him to find something to do. She wouldn't brush him away but she would treat him as if he was the one who had the solutions, and he did know that he had the solutions, but he didn't want them from himself. Strange, but that's how it was and he knew it. He couldn't get his aunt to huff like his mother, and he felt funny when he asked her for something he knew he had. With his mother it was different.

Today their aunt got a phone call in the middle of their lunch and while she was talking she was very very happy. She kept on smiling and nodding her head as if the person on the other end could really see her and she would turn to Ahmad and Habib and she would smile at them a very big smile. When she hung up, after the other person had hung up for sure, she told them that she had heard news about their father, that someone knew where he was and that his group was trying to negotiate with the other group. 'Negotiate' meant more than a hour, more than a week, more than two weeks. Their aunt didn't know how long 'negotiate' was, and for that they couldn't understand how come she was so happy. She tried to explain but it didn't work so she tried to convince them that they should be happy, and she did, by the sheer force of hope shoving reason out of the way. It worked for a while, a short while, and then things went back to how they were.

Today I heard Habib remind Ahmad of how they had met their aunt when their mother was alive. It took some time for Ahmad to remember, although he didn't remember that much. What he did remember was a black toy car he used to have. He didn't remember where it came from and Habib told him it was from her. Then Habib started telling Ahmad about all the things that annoy him about his aunt, things that Ahmad had noticed, not liked too much, but had not seen in the same way that Habib did. Later on when his brother went off to do his own thing he found himself annoyed about some of these things. Like her moustache. Like the way her forehead sweats when she is knitting. Like the way she breathes heavily sometimes. These things annoyed him for the next two days and then not as much.

But there was another thing his brother had said that he didn't think about at the time but now it passed through his head quite a lot: "When are we going to get out of this situation?" At first the question made him think about where else he could go to, but then he started to think about how his brother had said it; it was as if he was thinking about it all the time, and also, when he said it it didn't sound as if he was asking a question. And then after a while he was left with the word 'situation'. Ahmad had never thought of things in terms of a 'situation', so he tried to digest the word, but it was a bit like having eaten a stone, indigestible, but it was too late, he had already taken that word in.

Today Ahmad went to the mirror and started to look at himself and then he saw his teeth. He looked at his teeth and started thinking about all the things that he does with his teeth. He eats with them, he bites with them, he holds one end of a Lego piece while he pulls the other end, he keeps his tongue from coming out at night, he can bite really big animals if he was attacked and there are lots of other things he can do with them, but he doesn't want to think about them anymore so he goes to the balcony, looks down and sees how high the balcony is. Then he goes to his aunt and asks her what happens if somebody falls all the way down to the ground. When his aunt said that they would die he asked her what happens when somebody dies and she said that she didn't know. He asked her where would they go and she said that she wasn't sure. She was going to say that some people believed that they would go to a really nice place if they had been good in their life and a burning place if they weren't, but she thought that he was too young for that. Anyway, he was happy enough with her answer. It wasn't one of his mother's answers but he had felt her honesty.

Next morning Ahmad overheard his aunt on the phone, it was something that had to do with his father and what he remembered from the conversation was one word that stuck to his head. He didn't understand it but it was her tone when she said it. He tried to figure it out: 'tore'? From 'tear'? 'Tear' from the eye or 'tear' from to 'tear up'? Either way it doesn't sound very good. And then there was 'ture'. 'Tured'? 'Tured'? 'Tured'? So he went and asked his brother what does 'tortured' mean. His brother asked him where had he heard that word and he told him. His brother said "Oh", and that's all he said. Ahmad followed him around and asked him what it meant and again he said that he didn't know. Later on he saw his older brother cry while his aunt patted his hair. She said he had a tummy ache. Ahmad thought that he must have had a really bad tummy ache so he kept quite and then went away so that his brother wouldn't be embarrassed to be seen crying.

Of course there were other kids in the street who knew what that word meant and Ahmad found out, and before he put two and two together he went and told his brother. His brother realised that Ahmad hadn't made the link so he said "Oh yeah, now I remember what it means".

A couple of days later Ahmad got two and two to be four so he went to check it with his brother and his brother said that he doesn't know anything about his father. Neither did his aunt. He asked them again and he got the same casual answers. He then went away but there was something at the back of his mind that wasn't right, a bit like putting a couch in a kitchen. Why would anybody do that? It doesn't feel right until you tell me why you put the couch in the kitchen. Is it because we're having guests that like to sit only in the kitchen? Is it because you want to clean the rest of the house so you need to have it out of the way? Is it because you really promised somebody you would do it? If none of these then what is it? Tell me.

Six months now since Ahmad and Habib have moved in with their aunt. I'll tell you there's one thing I've noticed about Ahmad since he has come here. It's his walk. He doesn't rush into things anymore, and I'm not sure if that's a good thing. I also hear his thoughts sometimes and he's trying to figure out too much stuff. God help him though, every now and then he comes up with a couple of funny things. For the past two weeks he has decided that the worst thing people have is the telephone. It always brings trouble. He told this to his aunt and she said that things weren't like that a few years ago. Well, for him 'a few years ago' was longer than he could remember so that's no good to him. He wanted something for his moment and he wanted it now, he wanted it for this 'situation', now. His aunt didn't know what he was on about, she asked him what those other kids had been telling him. He said, "Nothing". At first she didn't know what to say, but then she told him to go and make himself busy. He got even more pissed off inside himself, especially that he didn't know who to blame for his 'situation'. It was one of those days, and those days were around more often now.

Today his aunt had visitors. These visitors saw Ahmad and Habib and went through the usual clichés about cuteness. There was another thing that happened. You know when adults assume that kids are too young to figure out some stuff? And you know when adults sometimes get careless around children and talk a little bit loud assuming that they can't hear? It was one of those. "It wasn't a bad disease that killed their mother, no, a sniper's bullet". Now his walk is going to be more lethargic, his body will be supporting a head that is trying to digest what it has heard.

He goes and tells his brother what he has heard and his brother shouts at him telling him that it isn't true and that he has made it up. Ahmad kept on saying that he was telling the truth until his brother barged in on the guests and shouted at his aunt. At first she didn't know what to say, but then she thought to herself that he was old enough to know the truth, plus it was too late, she knew she wasn't going to come up with a convincing lie. He broke down and he wouldn't let her console him. Ahmad stood by the door watching and hearing new sounds from his brother's chest. As he witnessed this scene he felt his head getting crowded.

There's another sentence he has to live with. Whenever his aunt gets really frustrated by something Ahmad and Habib did, she would lose her head and ask God, accusingly, why did he put her in that situation? In Ahmad's head there was not only his 'situation', but also hers.

For the next two days Habib has been narky and snappy with his brother, but then out of the blue Habib came over to Ahmad and gave him three of his best marbles and walked off without saying a word. Ahmad did not get up and follow his brother to thank him as he felt like doing, for he knew it would have embarrassed Habib, so he just left them in his hand, looked at them, and felt for his brother.

One day Ahmad looked at the telephone and asked it to ring and tell his aunt something good. He waited for at least an hour, and it didn't ring.

Today Ahmad was on the balcony. Standing there and every now and then he looked down to see how high their floor was, and then how far the ground was. His brother came out eating an apple and started looking down as well. He thought his brother was looking at something and so he casually looked down instead of asking Ahmad what he was looking at. After a few minutes he turned to Ahmad and asked him what he was looking at. Instead of answering Ahmad asked him what happens to people when they die. Habib just looked at him and said "Don't be stupid, don't be stupid", and then threw the rest of the apple on to the next

65

building. They both watched it fall onto the next building's third floor balcony. It was fun. There was nobody there. If there was they would have run inside and it would have been even more fun. Their aunt would have asked them what they were up to that they were so excited and they would have giggled and kept on saying, "Nothing, really, nothing".

During the last while Ahmad had been thinking about 'situations'. He had overheard an old man in the street saying something like "It's all one big situation", and Ahmad had been thinking about this sentence. He got the feeling that all these 'situations' made up for one big 'situation'. He thought about it, until he decided that he would wake up early next morning.

This morning Ahmad woke up earlier than everybody else. When I say everybody I mean his brother and his aunt. Anyway, he woke up before them just like he promised himself he would, and he even managed it without an alarm. He went to the toilet and had his little pee. Then he went to his room and sneaked out his best clothes. He put them on in the toilet, and then he did something he had not done since he had last seen his mother. He brushed his teeth even though he hadn't had any dreams where he had eaten anything. Then he looked at his teeth in the mirror and wondered if anybody was going to see them. He didn't know, but he was glad he brushed them anyway. Then he looked in the mirror and wondered whether he would look better in a moustache. He didn't know. Then he went to the kitchen and slowly made himself his favourite breakfast. It was very messy but still better than he thought it was going to come out. Then he cleaned after himself. When he finished he was happy that he had not made much noise. And now he was ready.

Ahmad's two front teeth are 4 cm apart. They're beautiful. They might be a bit yellow because he hasn't taken much care of them but they are still beautiful. They are his teeth. Slightly yellowish, but now they are 4 cm apart and about a meter away from his head. They are strong, but not so strong so as to compete with my pavement. Not from the sixth floor. The whole jaw, misplaced, severely deformed, all of it. And a big crack in his head, his brain spilling out, now there's more blood, more blood

66

everywhere. There will be screams when the first person discovers him. If it is an old man then there won't be screams but shuffling for words that have something to do with God, but eventually there will be screams.

Audrey Thomas

My roots are in the US but my branches are in Canada. I was born in western New York State. At 21, went to England and taught school in Birmingham, where the kids kept saying, "Please, Miss, speak English." Fell in love with an art student in the El Sombrero Coffee Bar, eventually got married and emigrated to Canada in 1959

Last year I visited Cork. The first night a man walked into my bedroom in the middle of the night. At first I thought it was my father's ghost as I was sure I had locked the door. Turned out to be a confused traveller who'd taken a drop too many. Nevertheless, I couldn't pick him out at breakfast. Maybe it was a ghost – a ghost who likes beer?

I'm divorced, live most of the time on an island (pop. 1004) have three grown-up daughters and two grandsons. I've written 13 books and lots of radio dramas. I like to travel and observe.

Volunteers

Audrey Thomas

("Any affliction becomes bearable, if it can be recast as a story."
Gerhard Köpf, *Papa's Suitcase*)

The fiddle orchestra was half-way through its set when a young man brought you in, you and two others. People were dancing off to the side, as they do, as I sometimes do when not just my feet but my whole body can't stay still. I had been watching two tall, long-limbed blonde girls and thinking, where do they spring from, these long-legged blondes, with their neat little midriffs, their belly buttons like naval oranges? They were smiling their perfect smiles and leaping gracefully up and down along with a couple of dozen lesser mortals – the inevitable Sixties guy with his eyes shut and his tie-dye trousers slipping down below the crack in his bum, the women dancing by themselves, the couples. Tonight, beside the main stage, there will be hundreds of dancers, barefoot on the grass. "A fair field full of folk, found I there..." It becomes a kind of possession; sometimes you're almost afraid you can't stop, that you will go on dancing like this forever, like that woman in *The Red Shoes.*

I had been watching the blondes and that's how I happened to see you come in, with the young man who was your minder, you and the other two. He urged you gently to sit down but you were having none of it – you wanted to be up and dancing. So the young man smiled and shrugged and you stumbled forward to join the dance. You danced as a bear might

69

dance, lumbering, awkward, heavy-footed, but on your foolish face was a look of pure delight. Several times you went right up to the giant speakers and tried to embrace them; several times you clapped your hands and gave a shouted grunt.

Once you wanted to go up on the stage but the young man gently danced you away. The fiddles were playing a jig; faster and faster the music went, faster and faster their fingers and bows. Some of the fiddlers were very young; one girl looked as young as eight or nine.

I stopped thinking about anything but you, playing the game we all play sometimes, a grown-up game, What Might Have Been, for I, not wishing such a burden thrust upon me, a burden such as you, took the easier road, decided "no."

If I hadn't done that, would I have brought you here? We would come on the bus. On the bus you are happy, smiling at everyone, saying "I'm a summer baby, I'm a summer baby" in your voice like the voice from the bottom of a well. But once here, you hang back a little – perhaps the crowds frighten you, perhaps you weren't so sure about having your hand stamped. Or maybe you like it, rub your fingers over the inked place so many times I have to tell you, gently of course, "Don't do that, Love, you'll rub the ink right off."

I show you the Lost and Found, hung with golden helium balloons in the shape of stars. If we should get separated, I say, but gently, so as not to worry you. If we should get separated look for the golden balloons, okay? Just tell the people your name and I'll come get you.

" Okay," you say, "Okay, Okey-Dokey."

It's a beautiful day, a cloudless blue sky stretched tight as a hospital sheet above English Bay. Hot, though. We are both wearing sunhats and loose long-sleeved shirts. I have on an anklet of little silver bells, a long summer skirt. Nigh-seh, you say, patting the flowers on my skirt, Nigh-seh, making two syllables of it, patting your approval. Your shirt is bright pink, your favourite colour.

(Have I mentioned a father in all this? Brothers or sisters?)

We used to live in the country, in a small town. I felt you would be more accepted there. Sometimes I was right and sometimes wrong. You can frighten people – you are excessive in your likes and dislikes, noisy, attention-seeking. At first you frightened the little children, even though you were a child yourself. Perhaps it was the mothers you frightened, really – children pick up on things like that – a certain look, a pulling away. A mother who is afraid of snakes will have a child afraid of snakes.

I dressed you every morning. "No, Love, that's your right foot, okay? Right foot, right shoe," saying a prayer of thanks for whoever invented velcro. I never got angry at you, having made that vow the moment I made my decision. But I am also thankful for the woodpile and the excuse for chopping, chopping, chopping. (You would like your red socks best.)

The little fiddler who looks about eight is so serious, so absorbed. I played the fiddle once, or rather, I played the violin. Tried to. My grandfather gave it to me in an old black wooden case. Once a week I went downtown to a music store that had lesson rooms on the second floor. I was never any good at it; I didn't practice and I was ashamed to be seen carrying that old-fashioned black wooden case. Now I listen to these children play and my fingers buzz.

"Never too late," says the man in charge, at the break. "I do teach those who are over nine; it's not as hard as it looks." But of course it is. Everything is as hard as it looks – sometimes harder.

For over an hour they've been announcing a child who's become separated from her grandmother. A lost child. "Will Alice please come to the Lost and Found, her grandmother is waiting for her there." I imagine the grandmother, allowed to take the child to the festival for the first time. She turns around and the child is gone. I imagine her panic – her daughter has put off having children – there will only be the one child, a lovely child, doted on but not spoiled, brought up to assume that the world is a loving place. The grandmother sits on a chair in the Lost and Found tent, watches as things pile up on the tables – hats, sunglasses, cameras, a red wallet, baby soothers, a small Swedish flag, a plush bunny with one ear. How long does she wait before they call the police? "A blue cotton dress," she will say, "covered in yellow flowers, a blue sunhat, jellies, no socks. She was there – and then she wasn't. We were crossing the wooden bridge, after the Little Folks Concert...Please..."

No one allowed to leave. 10,000 people here, at the very least. Is one of them an abductor of little girls in blue dresses?

71

(I would take you to the Little Folks Show. You clap long and loudly. Parents turn around, give you that "how sad" look, lean over suddenly to kiss the hair of their own, their perfect, children.)

On our street, two blocks down there was a baby with a big head. How did we know? His mother wheeled him out in a baby carriage with a thin but opaque veil of some cotton stuff hanging down so you couldn't see in. Every day, rain or shine, along our street and down Beethoven Street to the Austria bakery and coffee shop, where somebody always held the door open for her. She pushed the buggy to one of the tables at the very back and sat there for half an hour drinking coffee and reading the magazine she had brought with her. Then she came home, lifted the baby out (always covered by a shawl), went in the house and shut the door.

Ours was a friendly street. The women, the mothers, knocked on the door with offers of casseroles, babysitting, "anything you need." She shut the door in their faces, politely but firmly.

Because we never actually saw the baby he began to invade our dreams. A huge head, like a Martian – maybe he was a Martian baby! – something always pulsing at the top. Martian eyes. We knew about breast-feeding, although these were still the days when such a thing would never have occurred in public. Most of us younger ones had never even seen a mature breast unless covered up. Our mothers bottle-fed baby brothers and sisters yet we were sure this baby was breast-fed, imagined that great lolling head against its mother's breast, sucking away. We dared one another to sneak into the backyard and peer in the kitchen window.

Now I wonder if perhaps you and others like you or like that baby in my hometown, aren't really aliens, from another planet. Perhaps the alien seed scattered like the white hairs of dandelions and some of it went too far, travelled through galaxies until it came to rest in human wombs. Here, our gravity hinders and deforms you, our atmosphere gives you breathing problems. On your own planet you are beautiful, swift as young ponies, brilliant, able to solve elaborate equations in your heads. On your planet there is no need for sheltered workshops or special classes.

One day the family was gone. The Mayflower van arrived at breakfast on a Saturday and later, after the furniture and appliances, the family came out, the young mother with the baby parcelled up in shawls and blankets, the young father who worked as a golf pro at the Country Club. They got in their car and drove away and mostly we forgot about them. Hallowe'en was coming – we had other things to think about.

One of the women further down the block told my mother that the baby never cried, at least when it was in the buggy, which was sometimes left in the backyard if the weather was fine. "Imagine," said my mother. A baby who didn't cry was unnatural.

"They've gone to live with her parents," the woman said, "someplace down near Scranton, Pennsylvania."

I heard my mother talking to my father. "Better to let the poor thing die."

"Hmph," said my father from behind the evening paper.

In the sheltered workshop you sand bits of wood that become planters shaped like swans. You like doing this; it makes you feel important, useful. We have moved into the city so that you can be with some others more like you. The five year olds you knew when you were physically five have left you far behind; each year you must make new friends among that year's crop of five year olds. You run after your old playmates but they have other things to do now, Grade Two things, Grade Three, Grade Four. We find an apartment in the city. You go to the workshop on the bus, the same bus at the same time every weekday. You need that kind of order in your life. The bus driver knows you; when he takes his holidays he always makes sure the new driver knows your name. "Hello Louis, how's it goin?"

Each year we collect another swan planter and plant it with herbs and flowers. Our apartment is on the second floor, south-facing, and has a balcony – tiny but big enough for a container garden. The sprouting of seeds never ceases to amaze you. You love the fragrance of the herbs, the dazzle of marigolds and zinnias. Sometimes neighbours complain about your noise; sometimes I complain about theirs.

You learn to knit on big needles and present me with a long scarf, enough wool for a giraffe. I wear it proudly. "Red and yella" you say to me, "Red and yella, catch a fella." Margaret taught you that; Margaret is the director of the workshop.

Sometimes men flirt with me when I'm on my own, but I ignore them. After a while I take to wearing my grandmother's wedding ring. This puzzles you. Margaret is married, so are some of the helpers; you know what a wedding ring is. "Where is your father?" you say, mistaking the word. All husbands are fathers to you. Boys like you do not grow up to be fathers. I read that in a book. I read other things too, in the months after I made my decision. Why your tongue is the way it is, your head, your feet. The librarians oozed sympathy. I found out about the Simian line, I found out about the villain, Chromosome 21.

You cried very little at first; you were strangely floppy, almost boneless. I found out that all this was normal – for you.

Once I bring a man home, a friend I've met through work. But you wake up in the middle of the night – something has frightened you. You come down the hall, running heavily in your flat-footed way; you bang on my door. You are terribly upset. Is it jealousy? Are you afraid I will leave you? You sob and sob and refuse to be comforted.

I had not hidden the fact of you from my new friend; I would never do that. But I was stupid to think you wouldn't mind him in my bed.

"I'd better go," he whispers, as he comes out of the bedroom dressed, carrying his shoes. I nod over your head. He lets himself out.

Your father was married, always about to leave his wife, like a kid who has climbed to the highest diving board and stands there, afraid to look down, everyone yelling jump, jump, jump! No – just one person, me, yelling jump, jump, jump.

Folk Festival – *herrenvolk*. Hitler would have loved those blonde girls, but you?? He would have got rid of you quick.

The volunteers wear special tee-shirts: SITE CREW, GATE, SECURITY, PHOTOGRAPHY, PLATES. Would we volunteer for PLATES, stand side by side, wearing white plastic surgeon's gloves, each with a pile of new $2 coins in our right hand? As the customer drops the used plate in the bin and receives his money you call out "And the dish ran away with the spoon" over and over: "And the dish ran away with the spoon." Sometimes you drive me mad. Sometimes I just want to walk away from all of it, from you.

I was young; my chances were one in 2,300. Why me? "It is entirely up to you," the doctor said.

"What would you do?" I said, "if you were in my shoes."

He was honest with me. "I don't know."

He explained that there were degrees from mild to severe, a kind of Richter scale of retardedness. Later, in one of the books I read I learned that the old terms – idiot, imbecile, moron – had been replaced by Severe, Moderate, Mild. By age 18 "normal" for you would be 5 1/2 years.

"Perhaps you need some time to talk this over with your – ah, your – ah."

The doctor wasn't much older than I was.

"There is no 'ah," I said.

"I see."

I said to him what my father always said in a puzzling situation: "I see,' said the blind man as he took up his hammer and saw."

I went out into the waiting room and picked up a magazine, sat down again as though what had just happened hadn't really happened yet, that I was still waiting for my appointment. I read an article on "30 Thirty Minute Winter Stews", on "Safety in the Schoolyard". I read an advertisement for one of those limited edition plates which are supposed to Increase in Value twenty-fold, "complete with hand-numbered certificate of authenticity." I threw the magazine down and went out into the street.

A Sally Ann Santa was ringing his bell on the corner. I had a friend once who used to work as a department store Santa in the university vacation. He said he had to wear a rubber apron underneath his big, red baggy pants; the kids got so excited a lot of them peed on his lap.

"You see a kid crying on Santa's lap, he's not afraid of Santa, he's afraid of what his mother is going to say."

Would you want to go back and see Santa year after year? Could we find a Santa who wouldn't mind? Who would see that you were just a small boy in a large body? Would you have a row of Christmas-with-Santa pictures on your dresser?

What would you ask for? A puppy, I think; you would always ask for a puppy, no matter how many times I explained about puppies and apartments. Finally I get a kitten; you name her Blackie and nearly hug her to death. After it becomes a cat it knows how to keep out of the way of your rough loving.

"No fun," you say. "That cat is no fun." The next year you ask for a puppy.

During the day, knowing you are safe, I go out to work in a health food store called "Natural Selection". I tell them right at the beginning I can't do overtime – ever. We spend our evenings looking at books, watching movies on the VCR. You love the Three Stooges and animal films: Lassie, The Black Stallion or films like The Land Before Time.

When you are asleep I read my own books – we each select armloads of books from the library every week. And sometimes I just sit and cry. Silently, for my tears frighten you. You can have moods but me, never, or never in your company.

"The majority do not appear to develop a sexual drive to the same degree as ordinary people." I read that in a book as well. But enjoy cuddling, holding hands.

And some mentally handicapped people can fall in love. Will that happen to you? How will I feel about it? Relieved, because now I am no longer the exclusive object of your attention? Worried – how will they make a go of it? Who will rent to them? I circle classified ads; I do the rounds of landlords and landladies.

"Yes, my son and his fiancée – they are arriving soon." No mention of your condition, her condition. I wear neat, efficient-mother clothes, pantyhose and good shoes, not the jeans and shirt I wear at the Health Food store. I find a small apartment not too far away from mine and on the same bus route you've been used to all these years. Put down the first and last month's rent and a damage deposit. The landlord is delighted that I've found what I was looking for.

A volunteer, in a garden, is something that just sprang up – not something deliberately planted. Volunteers come out of the compost or are dropped by birds. Over the years I've discovered they are often the hardiest plants; they don't seem to wither, or fall prey to diseases at the same rate the other plants do. So you are not a true volunteer – you fall sick easily. In the old days, before the miracle drugs, you wouldn't have lived past thirty.

The music is coming to an end. I have been watching you, your joy –

so simple, so complete. Tears run down behind my dark glasses; people are standing up and stretching, clapping vigorously. I can't move. I sit here, tears run down behind my dark glasses – surprised by grief – such pain I want to double over and hold myself. I was young, I cry silently. I was young, my whole life was ahead of me. Please. Please understand. I'm sorry. I'm sorry Louis Rien.

I am here at the festival with two old friends from Quebec. Now they are standing, looking down at me, concerned.

"Marie," they say, "why are you crying? Pourquoi pleur-tu?"

Lisa Steppe

Born in Germany; studied English and German at Heidelberg and Munich Universities; taught for 15 years while annoying my employer (the Bavarian State) as a peace and anti-nuclear activist; left Germany to be reborn (together with the spring-lambs) in Ireland in 1984.

I live in the back of beyond in Yeats Country and when writing I try to smuggle the "blank page" into my short-stories (Tania Blixen calls it "the space that sings"). Published in Germany with 2 books, a children's book (shortlisted for the German Jugendbuchpreis) and a travelogue. Since 1994, I've been writing in English and won numerous prizes and awards, both in prose and poetry. Broadcast on RTE and NWR; published in anthologies and magazines (THE STINGING FLY, FORCE TEN, KALEIDOSCOPE).

Without Ireland I wouldn't have started to "sing" again. So homage to – my motherland.

Teller of Tales

Lisa Steppe

Sell out! Selling our ancestors to the pharma-freaks, selling our genealogy, our health records, our manias, our running berserk. They will manufacture the new miracle drugs, made up of Bjornsson's breakdown, his holing up in the refuge at Hlöthufjell.

I'm pacing up and down alongside my maps, hung out on all four walls of my kip, here in mean Copenhagen. A recluse like my father, crazy Bjornsson. Sometimes I stand still, rodentlike, watching out. Watching the stretch from Hlöthufjell to the River Far, washed out like a primary school wall, Hlöthufjell a blur. On leaflet 58, covering Lambahraun, fingerprints, the index finger grazing the long route to the River Far. The River Far. Walking the memory track again with Gloria Whitehand, walking the route in my mind, again and again.

The legend underneath is still readable, marking the island's civilised rind, central-heated, dotted with American-style bungalows. Indoors huge freezers, stacked with steaks and whale-meat chunks – while in the outdoors the black deserts bloom, black eruptions, sulphur-heat, jeep tracks in the deep, erring sand. And towards Vatnajökull, can you remember, we saw the camel-humped mounds, obscenely green in the black lavasand, housing the spirits of the land who can't be mopped up and sold. Not them.

They will track down Bjornsson's son as well and find me here, in mean Copenhagen, among Spiderwoman and my good old maps, the very best, up-to-date, holding it all, a holdall of green and black and fuming memory.

They say we'll get millions including free access to the natty drugs, drugs that encapsulate our history, the history of the FIVE BLACK CENTURIES. That's science. The cute little hoor. Inventive, isn't it?

But the real crime will be committed with our stories because we are the people who grow stories and eat books. They will upend our stories, sniff them out, compress them into tiny hankies of facts, categorize them.

Why do they feel so horny about our health records? Because we are an ethnically clean people. Not much intermarriage since the time of the first settlers. Ergo, we are the cradle of Europe, represent its roots. My dear, we represent the European, THE WHITE MAN. Maniacs. Butchers. Murderers. And now, science hopes to find a cure for our species. Ha.

The Langjökull glacier set the scenario for our story, winging down, pink like old Chinese silk. The ice-beast tongued the sand under which bloc-lava was hidden. Our wanderings had turned into a nightmare. There were deep crevices under the sand and I had to give you a hand when you suddenly went under, my proud schooner. We saw ice-mirages. Once our shadows were reflected on the Langjökull glacier like apocalyptic riders, inhumanly gigantic and fear lunged at you, my girl from the Bronx, made your white hands flutter in the thin, cruel air. It was then that I told you parts of THE ICELAND BELL, told you about Snaefridur-Whitehand, renamed you.

"See," I said, "this is your native country from where your parents emigrated to America: ice, fire, sand. And don't you forget Iceland's demon lovers – the glacier rivers, child-like in the morning and devouring hags in the evening."

It was seven hours later, midsummernight, the sun set in the white sheet of the sky, streaked like a toy-marble, when we found the indentation of our bodies where we had lain hours before. You said, your voice a croak: "I wished I had never laid my eyes on you."

But it was too late.

You had it all wrong, right from the beginning and I, right from the beginning, knew it. I knew you would be mine.

When we started out from Reykjavik, you didn't know much about Iceland – only The Five Black Centuries your parents had to learn by heart in school. Decimation of the population by the plague, eruptions, hard winters, famine, marauding English hordes and finally the inferno of Lakagigar when it broke out in 1783. Your parents told you that the sheer mass of the erupting lava was the largest one recorded in human history and that it could be seen as far as Africa and Asia. But I didn't want to trace back history, though you were eager to learn about your 'roots'. You were curious. But the land forbids curiosity. Its elemental giants will stand up and have their own say. Here, even the air is an enemy, inscrutable. An eternal warfare, that's Iceland.

And when they try to make it accessible for American tourists, the cargoes safely stowed away in Range Rovers, labelled NORTHERN EXPLORER, OPERATION HELLHOLE, VOLCANO EXPRESS – that's not Iceland. That's TV.

I didn't want to trace back your roots with you – though you had hoped we would go down to Hvolsvöllür where your mother's lineage came from. What I wanted was to include you in my COLLECTED STORIES.

Stories keep us going, they are our lifeline. More than most nations we are captives of the written word. Even in the most desolate times, the written word kept casting a spell on us .

I quoted Laxness to you – our Nobel Prize Winner – you hadn't even heard his name, let alone read him. I told you everything. I told you about my father who was kept prisoner in the refuge we had slept in – trapped by his own crazy mind.

I made you stop setting your footsteps into mine, your trainers so firmly planted on deep, loose, wicked sand. I held you against my body, your blue-white, striped cotton shirt open. You didn't wear a bra. Your white breasts were covered in sweat, sandsperm glistened on your skin. You were very pale. I wanted you like that, half naked – a white aborigine.

I had met you at Kevlavik Airport, an American tourist with a canary-yellow rucksack.

The airport is my natural haunt. Here I get to know people, that is women. Seed for my stories.

You were flirtatious, bold, fooling around with two stupid guys in the

81

bar. You pushed the taller one off the stool, your eyes ablaze with merriment.

This ridiculous horseplay went on for at least half an hour. I watched you.

Then you got up to join the boys for a taxi ride into Reykjavik. I intervened. I approached you.

"Excuse me, you left your book behind."

"My book?" You shook your head.

"The Njall Saga."

Your eyes widened. "I've never come across that title, never owned a book like that. What did you say? Njall Saga?"

"That means you haven't a clue who Hallgerdur is," I said and wagged my index finger.

We both burst into laughter.

"So that's how you Icelanders hook us American girls?"

"Well, it might interest you as an American woman that Hallgerdur was the first feminist in history. When her husband Thorvaldur slapped her face, she had him killed by her father."

Your white shoulders haven't seen much sun lately. How come?

Snow on Mt. Kilimanjaro.

Your head is on the pillow, your right knee is crossed over the left, bent knee. The leg dangles in mid-air, child-like, it dimples the skin of the upper calf. You are wriggling on the mattress, giggling.

I try to catch your right footsole with a fast, whiplike tongue. Lizard-tongue.

You scream with pleasure, "Nooooo."

You want more.

Later I comb your blonde, explosive hair, all curls and revolution. Angela Davis posing as Blondie. You still smell of your last shower in the US. A perfumed shower. Good stuff. I suck you. I eat you.

We are in the refuge, at the Hlöthufjell. Tomorrow we will set out for Lambahraun, the Far...

I call what we are doing a SAFARI. You just love that, a real Icelandic safari. I whisper the names of Safaris like endearments in your ear:

VOLCANO EXPRESS. OPERATION HELLHOLE. I tell you I had been a Safari-guide for years. You are happy. You get the real thing.

Leaflet 58 (Discovery series); scale 1:100 000
    The vastness of Lambahraun. Later the track bolts through the Gap. From there, through stone desert – to the River Far.
    The relief is laid out in contour intervals; black lines and interrupted black lines. Black dots – culminating points. The assertive red line of our route. It ends abruptly.

    "I'm sorry, I forgot to put the rope in the rucksack."
    "What?"
    "I would have needed it when we cross the Far. Normally the guide is tied up with the rest of the group. It's like in the mountains when you traverse glacier fields."
    "But you didn't tell me we would have to walk the ice."
    "We don't. But the Far is a glacier river. After a hot day, it can ride up to your breast."
    "Why? Is there no bridge?"

After we made love on the mattress in the refuge, under the blackened rafters that gleamed above our heads – one spot up there was dulled, the paint scraped off – I prepared dinner. I had brought along dried shark's meat. Ethnic food. I thought you would like it. The real thing, as you called it.
    From the corner of my eye I watched you handling the stones you had collected. They were covered with emerald fungus. You lined them up in a row, picked one, rubbed it against your cheek, eyes closed, an angelic smile on your face. You breathed in deeply.
    "Are you trying to breathe in stone?"
    You opened your eyes. "It's pulsating. It HAS a heart."
    "I'm not so sure about that."
    "Everything is alive," you declared.
    "So you mean I'm alive, too?"
    You are still confused by my mercurial ways. On the other hand, you

83

have that notion that this is the real thing as well. Me – a man with a twisted mind. Truly Icelandic.

"You are an awful joker." Your head lies on my chest. When you embrace, you cling. I like that.

"Sometimes we can't relate well." I hear your schoolgirl's voice. "I guess, it's the generation-gap because you are twenty years older. You could be my Dad."

"Wrong," I tell Gloria Burton, "I'm not twenty years older. I came here a thousand years ago with the Norwegians, with Ingolfur and his brother Leifur. I was one of the Irish slaves, they had brought along with them. I helped to kill Leifur. After the murder, we fled to the Vestmannaeryjar islands…"

"Oh," you pout your lips. "You talk about reincarnation."

"No, Love, I simply crack a joke."

What infuriates me: my health records – or ill-health records – are still with the health board in Reykjavik. I can't lay my hands on them, destroy them. All I can do is rant away, pacing up and down along my walls watching out for leaflet 58, in case there is a change. Somebody has started to scratch the surface off the map between the Gap and the Far. What is HE up to? What is Bjornsson's son up to?

I rummage in my kitchen table drawer, look for my Collected Stories. SALLY. JENNIFER. JOAN. VIN. GLORIA WHITEHAND. I brought them all out to the hut at the foot of the Hlöthufjell, slept with them under the blackened rafter my father hanged himself from. After that, the Far…So, all my stories have some elements in common, and yet, are unique. Gloria's story is exceptional, though. She put up a ferocious fight. She didn't wade into the Far voluntarily. I had to push her in. I had never done that before. Afterwards I went undergound, disappeared in mean Copenhagen.

Your white shoulders are sunburnt. Your burnt, scaly hands tremble when you hold the cigarette paper between thumb and ringfinger. You lick the paper. You don't look me in the eye anymore. But you can't run away either. You silently smoke your cigarette staring at a point in the distance:

in the centre of the glacier, a black mass squats, emanating a lurid presence. A nameless mountain. The legend only marks its height. 999 metres. I don't tell you "that's the heart of darkness" because you are the only one who already KNOWS. I've never experienced a woman like you, Gloria. Within two days you changed beyond recognition. You turned into an animal. I had to remind myself that it had only been two days ago when I rubbed Hart's Balm into your sore feet. I didn't tell you then it was crazy to set out for Iceland's wilderness in white trainers.

Now we sit here, finally facing THE RIVER, you smoking your cigarette. The Far is yellow, like your rucksack, feverish, hallucinating, thrusting between the flat sandbanks, its meltwater rides a hellish current.

I have already removed your passport from the side-pocket of your rucksack. There is a small linen pouch strapped to your left shoulder. It contains your traveller cheques. I remove that as well. You don't remonstrate. You breathed in stone and now you are stone.

You don't move. You prepare for the fight. You will take me by surprise and nearly take me with you.

"To destroy the husk – in order to immortalize, to memorize in a story."

I had always managed to stay philosophical and pleasant right to the end and the chosen woman had waded into the river, trusting me, her guide. I would give her instructions to serve my purpose.

"Pull the rucksack's hip-belt tight."

Wrong. She won't slip out of the rucksack when the current uproots her and sweeps her along.

I don't give YOU any instructions. Funny thing: I don't dare. You keep on smoking. You have grown up the last two days. You made a quantum leap.

Now you are eerily quiet, intense.

Your presence is everywhere.

The current is delirious.

Melissa Gaskill

Growing up in Texas, writer Melissa Gaskill spent many summer hours on the Llano River, the scene of her short story.

A professional writer for 18 years, Gaskill has had articles in many publications, some of them obscure but most notable among them the *Austin American Statesman, Dallas Morning News, San Antonio Express News, Modern Maturity, American Way, Family Fun, Texas Business and Texas Highways*. She has won awards for journalism, script writing and short fiction. Her greatest accomplishments, however, are her three children, ages 12, 9 and 6. While placing nearly insurmountable physical limitations on her ability to write, their presence has enhanced her creativity and maturity immeasurably. She lives in Austin, Texas, with her husband and children.

Swift Water

Melissa Gaskill

That warm May day in 1968, Delia Mason almost didn't go to the river. The soda machine needed restocking and she hadn't finished last month's books, there were new shower curtains to hang, her freezer to defrost, and wash piling up. Time to go to town for groceries.

After breakfast, she watered her patch of scrawny tomatoes and perpetually thirsty bean vines, and stuck a couple of ripe tomatoes in the pockets of the apron she had forgotten to remove. Walking back to the house, she stopped off at the pumphouse to wash a load of laundry.

The twenty rooms of the Parker Motel stretched like gangly arms from either side of a plain, boxy house. Inside the house, an old metal desk served as the motel office. Someone always had to watch that desk. This morning, Delia's father, Harland Brown, sat behind it while her husband Ed cleaned motel rooms.

When Delia walked in, Harland jumped up and turned off the television. He had opposed Ed's purchase of their four-story antenna, and to be caught watching the stations that came through it must seem like admitting Ed had been right.

Her father, who owned the motel, and her husband, who ran it, argued over everything. Delia walked a tightrope in the middle.

"Mornin's been pretty quiet," her father reported.

"Tuesdays usually are." Just three rooms last night. Two more tonight. Slow. Number 4 needed a new air conditioner and the roof over Number

11 leaked. Delia hoped to fill more rooms on the weekend.

She went into the kitchen and took three blue plates from the cabinet. She called to her father, "You staying to eat?"

"I reckon. You got enough to go around?" Harland and Mattie lived in a tiny trailer at the end of the motel opposite Delia's garden. Her parents seldom cooked, making the short walk to her kitchen instead.

"We'll manage." Delia added another blue and a yellow plate to her stack. She closed the cabinet door with a glance at the lone yellow plate left on the shelf.

Alex burst through the kitchen door, his face flushed and burrs stuck in his white socks. After a recent growth spurt, his legs looked too skinny to support the rest of his eight-year-old body.

"Dinner ready? I'm starved."

"Nope. Another hour yet." Delia set the plates on the table.

"Call me when it's ready." Alex dashed back out the door and Delia shook her head. That boy never walked anywhere he could run, never slowed down for a hug anymore. She tore open a package of ground meat and crumbled it into a bowl for meatloaf.

Her mother came in the back door, peered into the still-empty oven, then went in the den and turned the TV back on without a word. Mattie had never been much on small talk.

Delia slid the oversized meatloaf into the oven and took the tomatoes from her pocket to wash. Through the kitchen window, she looked out at the highway where the world sped by on its way from one place to another. The trucks got bigger and the cars faster, but the Parker Motel, her oasis, never changed.

The family took their usual places around the faded linoleum and Delia set out iced tea. Five heads bowed and Ed let out a loud breath before quickly reciting the short prayer he said at every meal.

The 'Amen' barely out of his mouth, Ed reached for a piece of bread and slathered it with margarine. "Sure is getting hot out, and not even June. Folks'll be wanting to swim in this heat. May be the year to put in that pool."

Harland snorted.

Delia passed the sugar bowl to her mother and gave Ed a withering look. The same old argument. Ed: a swimming pool would be good for business, pay for itself in five years. Daddy: pools were a waste of money with the lake across the highway and the river two miles away. Neither one of them ever budged, or gave up on the subject. Once they almost came to blows.

Delia loved pools herself, but didn't want to force anyone to choose.

"Yeah, a pool would be neat." Alex swirled his bread around his plate in an unconscious imitation of his father. "Steve's folks put in one of those above ground kind. It's deep enough to dive in."

Delia looked at him in disbelief. "Dive in! It doesn't look all that deep to me." As she recalled, that pool only came up to her chin, with no diving board.

She spooned green beans onto Alex's plate and passed Ed a second helping of meatloaf. For a few minutes the only sound came from forks clicking on plates and a few cats mewing out back.

"Well, it is hot enough to go swimming." A small man and therefore a light eater, Harland finished first. "And we don't need a pool to do that." He shot a glance at Ed, who ignored it. Harland turned to Alex. "Reckon you could talk your Momma into a trip to the river?"

Alex's eyes lit up. "Could we, Mom?"

"You go ahead. I'm done cleaning rooms, I can watch the office," Ed said.

Delia bit her lip, thinking about the shower curtains, the freezer, the books. Well, those things would keep one more afternoon. Sometimes a body really needed to feel cool water.

The Llano River wanders through the Texas hill country, spreading several hundred yards across, a varied and fascinating thing. Dozens of streams thread among granite rocks that litter the wide riverbed as if God spilled a load of them on His way somewhere else. Gurgling rapids drop from deep pools into wide, sandy expanses barely ankle deep. Banks and hills of reddish sand collect among the rocks and water, and wild grasses and scruffy mesquite trees take hold wherever they can.

Delia loved water. She especially loved this river, and came to it often. Sometimes she simply sat on a rock, the water flowing around her ankles like cool caresses. Occasionally, she dangled a fishing pole in the water as an excuse for sitting there. When her baby girl died without ever taking a breath, Delia brought her ache to the river. Her body bore no outward mark, only horrible scars inside. She prayed the rapids would wash those scars away, and when they didn't, imagined floating away on the water like a broken stick.

Whenever she crested the hill and saw the river spread out before her, something inside Delia quieted.

Harland parked under a shade tree next to the low water crossing several miles from the motel. Alex spilled from the car and darted to watch the water rush from under the bridge. High from recent rains, the rapids foamed white, rushing through the boulders.

Delia folded a towel under her and sat on a smooth curve of granite. Alex leaped into a pool of water, dragging an old inner tube. Harland watched his grandson from the junction of rock and water, a battered hat pulled low over his eyes.

"Stay away from the bridge!" Delia called as Alex clambered up some rocks, lugging his tire to the top of a set of rapids.

Over and over, Alex shot down the rapids on the tube and climbed back to the top, until Delia felt exhausted just watching him. Finally, he plopped down on a spread of sand to dig with a stick. Delia tried not to imagine a second blond head bent over next to his, another pair of sandy hands. She leaned back and closed her eyes, about to doze off, when a sudden commotion brought her to her feet.

A knot of people stood where the river squeezed through a narrow opening and shot out the other side of the bridge. A frantic woman struggled in the grip of a large man, screaming.

"He's trapped in there! Let me go!"

Two fellows waist deep in the water clutched the side of the bridge, reaching underneath it. As Delia moved closer, she saw they were just boys. She waded into the water, then stopped when someone on the other side shouted, "There he is!"

She splashed to the bridge and rushed across. A small body in red swim trunks tumbled through the rapids and partly onto a sand bank, then floated away, bobbing up and down in the water. The boys rushed toward the red trunks, and the woman broke loose and clambered into the rapids, shoes and all. Harland hurried after her. Delia fell into the frantic parade, moving as fast as she could, the rocks sharp on her bare feet.

She pushed her thin legs through the water, wanting to reach out and grasp everything precious to her, to keep it safe. To snatch that boy from the water and out of danger. She moved faster, her eyes on the others scrambling to catch the red speck bobbing in the river.

"Mom! Momma!"

Alex's voice stopped her. She'd forgotten him, for just a minute. On shaky legs she made her way to the bridge, stumbling on the rocks.

Alex grabbed her hand. "Will they get him out?"

Delia looked at his face, crinkled with concern, and wondered how much truth a boy ought to know about a thing like safety.

"They'll get him out –" Her voice failed her. She looked back down the river as a figure lifted a small, limp body, the red trunks like a warning beacon on a distant shore.

Delia turned to a young man on the bridge. "Do you have a car?"

He nodded.

"Run to it. Drive to that house at the turnoff." She pointed up the hill. "Tell them to call the ambulance in Kingsland. Hurry."

He ran.

The people in the water picked their way back, bent and beaten. The woman, dress wet to the waist and shoes gone, held a lifeless hand in one of hers. Harland held her other hand.

They watched the ambulance driver and helper carry the boy to the open vehicle, his body leaving dark, wet stains on their white clothes. The ambulance drove away in wrenching silence.

The boys and mother went to their car, climbed into the stifling, closed-up heat. Delia shuddered and breathed deeply of the open air.

"They were out here on a vacation from Lubbock, staying at the Lodges," Harland said. "The fellow who caught him is one of his big brothers. Said the boy was a good swimmer, but never been in a fast river like this."

They drove home without conversation. Delia watched Alex stare out the window, his usual chatter stilled, and her own mind went blank where

91

words of comfort should have been. She thought of being pregnant, a too-fragile vessel carrying precious cargo. A life inside of her, riding in the car and crossing the street whenever she did. Then that life out in the world and even harder to protect.

Pain washed over Delia like foaming rapids. She hadn't even been able to keep Ann safe inside her. And now this awful reminder that she couldn't keep Alex safe on the outside.

Everything is our responsibility, but so much of it is out of our hands. Careless drivers, viruses, mean people, swift water. What if it had been Alex caught under that bridge?

Delia closed her eyes. A casserole. When someone died, people made casseroles. They'd need something to eat, probably wouldn't feel like going out. Shoot, she could take a whole supper over there. The least she could do.

Harland parked the car and they climbed out, still silent.

Ed looked surprised to see them.

"Back so soon? I figured you'd pick up barbecue sandwiches and get back just in time to keep me from starving tonight." The smile on his face faded when he saw the look in Delia's eyes.

"You go clean up," Delia said to Alex. He twisted up his mouth but went without protest.

In the kitchen, Delia took out her best casserole dish and opened the refrigerator to see what she had to work with. Her hands shook.

"Reckon I'll go on down and see if your mother needs anything." Harland had one hand on the door. "Wouldn't want her to hear the news from someone else."

"Come on down for some cards after supper," Ed said. The men could always call a truce over a deck of cards. Ed turned to Delia as the screen door slammed. "What news?"

Delia took rice from the cabinet. She'd make a cake, too.

"A boy drowned at the Slab," she said without looking at Ed. "Went under the bridge, one of those narrow spots, and got stuck under there. He washed out the other side, but it was too late. Alex saw the whole thing."

Ed took her hands in his, stilling them. "Lordamighty. I figured the river would be high. Ought not to go again until it gets down a bit."

"But Alex has so much fun on the rapids. And everything is so beautiful when the water's really flowing." Her voice trailed off.

"Anybody we know?"

Delia shook her head. "I just wish Alex hadn't seen it." She remembered Alex's questions about Ann, his crayon drawings of a sister he never saw. His silence on the way home.

Ed gave her hands a gentle squeeze. "He'll be all right. He knows these things happen."

She sighed. "But seeing it right there in front of you. What if he gets afraid of the river or something?"

"Well, then, we'll just have to put in that damn pool so he can swim here. Hire a lifeguard so you won't worry." Ed grinned and Delia tried to smile back, wishing it were as simple as hiring a lifeguard.

Alex walked in wearing a clean T-shirt, shorts and a worn pair of sneakers without socks. "Mom, can we still get barbecue for dinner?" He looked at their hands locked together and rolled his eyes.

Ed laughed, squeezed Delia's hands again, then let them go. He ruffled Alex's hair.

"Looks like your mother already has plans."

Delia looked at the food on the counter. "Oh. No. This is for them, for the family." She glanced at Alex, then Ed. "They'll be hungry, I reckon. It's the least we can do."

Ed met Delia's eyes. "Do you want me to take it over for you?"

"No." She squared her shoulders. "I can do it. I want to."

Ed turned to Alex. "Then the answer is yes. Let's go buy us some supper."

She watched as they walked to the car, Ed's big arm draped over the skinny shoulders of a boy half his size. She fought back the urge to run after them as they climbed into the car, to call out *Don't go, it might be dangerous.*

Instead, she got a dime out of the desk and headed for the soda machine. Cooking always made her thirsty. She stood, the cold, hard bottle in her hand, watching the car disappear over the hill.

She leaned against the rough brick wall, the soda pressed against her hot cheek. The clear, wrenching memory of holding her tiny, perfect baby, still as a porcelain doll, caused her knees to buckle. Something like today could happen to Alex. It would be too much.

Her throat too tight to swallow the Dr. Pepper, Delia put the barely touched bottle in the wooden crates stacked beside the machine. She sat down. Her arms ached for the four-year-old girl she should be holding, and the boy who didn't want her to anymore.

It was almost dark when Delia pulled into The Lodges' driveway. In a box on the seat beside her sat a hot casserole, rice, home-grown tomatoes, a chocolate cake and four cold Dr. Peppers. Across the drive stood an above-ground pool, bathed in lights. The surface of the water shimmered, still disturbed by recent swimmers. Delia went into the office.

Behind the counter stood a tall, heavy woman, her hair bleached out by pool chlorine. "Why, hello, Delia. What brings you here this time of night?"

"Evening, Wanda. I brought a meal over for those folks from Lubbock. We were at the Slab today."

Wanda's smile turned down and she made tsk, tsk noises. "Terrible business, ain't it? Norman told us about it, when he brought them back from the funeral home in his patrol car." Wanda leaned over the counter, lowering her voice. "Do you know they're going to drive that boy to Lubbock themselves, put the coffin right in the back of that station wagon? Instead of let Ricky do it in his hearse? Have you ever heard such a thing?" Her small eyes opened as wide as they could go, no bigger than pennies.

Delia shifted her feet. "Well. Could you tell me what cabin they're in? I got food out there getting cold."

Wanda straightened up, studying Delia. "Now, that was a right fine thing of you to do. Wonder why I didn't think of that. Cabin 6. All the lights is probably still on. Norman had to take a statement, rule it accidental. And Ricky from the funeral home made a bunch of calls, trying to find out if what they was planning to do was all right. Never heard of anybody doing that, and I reckon..."

"Ummm. Thanks so much, Wanda." Delia backed out the door and gulped the night air. The lights blazed in Cabin 6. She parked next to the same car she'd seen at the river.

She knocked, her heart pounding, and recognized the boy that opened the door, clothes dry now, hair neatly combed.

"I'm sorry to bother you. I was at the river today, I couldn't help but see, that was my Daddy that helped you out of the water. I thought you all might be hungry, there's casserole and some fresh tomatoes, a cake, chocolate. Oh, now." Delia stuck out her hand. "Listen to me babble on. I'm Delia Mason. From the Parker Motel over on Highway 90."

"John Allbright." The eyes that studied her were red and tired, but the hand gripped hers firmly. "I'm Jimmy's big brother."

"Jimmy?"

"Yes. That's his name, my little brother." His voice choked.

"Oh, my stars." Delia realized the other people in the cabin were silent, staring at her. She collected herself. "Like I said, I've got supper for you, in the car."

The other young man came forward. "Let me help you. That's right thoughtful of you, Mrs. Mason, did you say it was?"

"Oh, call me Delia, please. And it's the least I could do, I mean..." her voice trailed off. Her eyes met the woman's. Delia recognized the pain in them, and almost took a step backward.

"It's still mighty kind of you." The woman had a soft, husky West Texas drawl. "All this happening so far from home. Everyone's so kind." Her eyes glistened and the boys moved to her side. She shook them off. "Go on, help Mrs. Mason with her things. I'm sure she has a home to get back to." She turned to the man sitting behind her. "Marion, clear off that table. This angel has brought us some supper."

At the sound of his wife's voice, the man jumped up like he'd been stung and awkwardly moved things off the table.

The woman turned back to Delia.

"I'm Louise Allbright, that's my husband Marion. You met my boys, John and Joe, he's the dark-headed one. And my Jimmy –" Tears spilled down her cheeks. Delia stepped into the cabin and put her arms around Louise, who began to sob.

"You go on and have a good cry." Delia whispered, patting Louise's back. The boys carried the box in, stepping around the women, their faces wary. Delia led Louise gently to the other side of the table and helped her sit. She pulled an opener from her apron pocket, popped the cap off a Dr. Pepper and put the bottle in Louise's hand.

"Drink this. You'll feel better."

Louise obediently drank.

The boys hovered at the smell of meat and chocolate.

"Why, you must be starving." Delia turned to a counter against the wall and pulled out plastic plates and a fistful of bent forks from a drawer. Not finding a knife, she stabbed the casserole with one of the forks, several times across the top, wiggling the handle until a chunk came loose.

Delia filled four plates with the casserole and rice and the boys immediately dug in. She set tomatoes on the table, wishing she'd brought salt.

"This is delicious, ma'am," the oldest boy managed between bites. His younger brother nodded. Delia smiled. Poor things, probably about faint from hunger, but not saying anything, not wanting to think of their own needs.

She looked down at Louise, who ate delicately.

Delia took a deep swallow of air. Here in this room breathed her worst fear. Yet these people still ate supper, remembered their manners. She saw real pain in their eyes, but it hadn't caused them to disappear from the face of the earth, explode into nothingness. Why, Louise even smiled when she took the Dr. Pepper.

Delia remembered this kind of pain. Her pain now felt different, duller. She could keep on breathing, talking, right through it. These folks would get there. One day they'd talk about Jimmy and not even cry. But they'd never forget him. She wouldn't. Just like she'd never forget her baby.

Delia filled the battered coffee pot with water, spooned in coffee and plugged it in. The percolator gurgled softly and the aroma of coffee began to fill the small room. Delia sliced the cake with the handle of a fork, and the boys held out their plates with shy smiles. Once, Delia would have thought it terrible, to see them smiling, their brother not dead a day. Now she knew better. Let them smile. Heck, let them laugh. She'd like to make them laugh. Mourning didn't bring someone back.

Delia set a matchbook on the table next to Louise. "Here's our number and address. You let me know if there's anything we can do."

Louise looked into her eyes, and Delia saw gratitude there, too. "You've done so much already."

"Why, cooked a sorry little meal is all. Wasn't anything."

"Oh but it was. So much more." Louise took Delia's hand. "You came. You cared."

Under her gaze, Delia looked down, uncomfortable.

"Well, I swear, you do make the best chocolate cake." The oldest boy had finished his piece.

"Joe, don't swear." Louise let go of Delia's hand. "You'll have to give me the recipe, if he likes it that much."

"It's coffee."

Louise glanced at the coffee pot, looked puzzled.

"Two tablespoons of coffee, in the cake, along with the chocolate. Brewed coffee."

"Oh." Louise actually laughed. A small one, but a laugh. Then she picked up the matchbook and slipped it into her pocket.

Delia put the empty dishes back into the box. "Just leave that cake plate here and I can get it later."

Louise stood and they hugged, and it felt as natural to Delia as if she'd known Louise all her life.

Driving home in the dark, Delia felt the tightness around her heart loosening. It hadn't been easy facing that family, their terrible loss, but it had been right. People help each other.

She pictured each of their faces in turn. Those boys would think they were taking care of Louise, but she had strength. Maybe everyone found strength eventually. Delia knew she had. She'd kept going. More than that. She'd finally been strong enough to help someone else.

The motel came into view, its neon sign aglow, red and blue, in the middle of a string of twenty yellow porch lights. Pretty as Christmas. She turned into the drive.

97

Robin Winick

Lives in suburban Connecticut, from which she is constantly trying to escape, sometimes with her husband and children to remote areas in Maine, Wales, or Ireland, where she has a fear of sinking in a bog. Her consolation would be that whatever manuscript she had on her would be preserved. Her other escape is writing, spotting the extraordinary among the seemingly mundane. Along with her brother she invented "Politics as Usual", a satirical game based on US congressional politics. Her short story "Cosgrave's Dilemma" was short-listed in the Fish Prize last year, and went on to win the Glimmer Train Prize.

Mrs Purvis

Robin Winick

Surely in such an uncertain world the two tiny acres would shrink; yes, they would shrink until she weaved and tottered on the head of a pin. She had told Mr. Purvis of this inevitability and of the more immediate problem of the noise and confusion and daily insinuations of the neighbors and their pets; but Mr. Purvis had quieted her remonstrances with the unmistakable hint in his voice that his irascible nature might manifest itself at any moment, if she were to continue. She sat, sipping her coffee by the kitchen window, nostalgic for the cold silent winter when the world was white and pure and clear and silent. In winter she would walk through the snow in the woods behind her house and admire the naked trees stark against the grey sky. She would inhale the cool air and sense it rushing through her body, purifying it; but now for the next six months her nostrils would clog with the rich vegetative odours of her lascivious plants, and she would be profaned.

Over night the leaves had returned to the trees in great unruly clusters, the azaleas had become obscenely full-bellied, cherry trees wept over emerald tufts of onion grass, and profusions of dandelions littered the lawn. Oh, the world was shrinking again; and the air so thick with spring she could hardly breathe. The men would come in dirty rusted pickups with all manner of rakes, spades, burlap and blowers and take over the property, blaring music, leaving sandwich wrappers about; and then there would follow the pesticide application; a sick sweet odour would rise in the air and ride on the breeze through the open windows to assault her senses and wipe out her brain cells.

By mid morning the tumult began. She peeked out of a window to find a truckload of gardeners at work, taming her lawn and garden. No doubt Mr. Purvis was trying to please her, but he had only doubled her agony by introducing the discordant human element. She dressed quickly and went outside to tell the men they must pack up immediately. The truck was an eye-sore and the noise, the cacophony of machinery, singing and radio music was going to set her delicate, fine-tuned nerve circuitry back months and months. Her psychiatrist would be appalled at this gross insinuation. Oh, men never thought about consequences, did they? she asked herself, and then she answered: especially Mr. Purvis.

As she strutted down the path, she drew from her pocket a little round pill and popped it into her mouth. Ah, the relaxation pill! On an empty stomach it would act quick and efficiently.

"You must go immediately," she told them politely. She liked words spoken coolly, crisply, clip, clip, as the British spoke.

"But we have been hired for the day," one replied.

Mrs. Purvis disliked his accent; the words came out thick, as if he were chewing a chunk of stale bread. She wondered about his origins and why Mr. Purvis could not have just hired good old Puritan stock, people with whom she could communicate easily, who would understand her delicate sensibilities.

"Then you may take the day off," she proposed.

"But you don't understand…"

There it was: the assumption. "But I do. Everyone deserves a day off, and of course, I will pay you just the same. I'll get my purse," she said, thinking, oh, yes, and a second pill.

"We will not take money for doing nothing," a short muscular man asserted, wiping perspiration from his face with a dirty cloth. "We are in America now."

"Of course you will; it's called charity here and really quite respectable. Instead of donating to some unseen hand, Mr. Purvis and I will simply give to you." As she turned to go back to the house, she felt a warm damp hand on her arm. It would leave a fine film of soil dust, she mused. The hand pressed into her, as if its owner were hoping an indelible print might remain when it was finally withdrawn; and she thought how life moves inexorably forward in such a way that no act or thought can be retracted. She had been tattooed.

"We do not take charity. We will stay until the job is complete." Retracting his large hand, the short muscular one looked up at his two colleagues, who nodded obligingly.

"But this is my property; shouldn't I have a say?" And then she thanked God for the relaxation pill. Otherwise, she might have sounded shrill, as if she had no patience, as if she didn't like these people. Then they would have surmised it was about ethnicity and not about the fact that she was averse to anyone or anything that disturbed the tranquillity of her life. Just when Mr. Purvis was off to God-knows-where, they came, but they would be gone tomorrow; so she relinquished her stand and retreated to the house, removed her shoes at the door and tripped across her spongy white rug to the kitchen, where she poured herself some soothing camomile tea. After the tea, she sank into her sofa and dreamed that it was the morrow and they were gone.

But the next day she awoke to their familiar sounds. She drew back the curtains and watched the men weeding and digging. Three azalea plants sat on the lawn waiting to be plunged into the earth. The bare sweaty backs of the men emitted a raw animal scent that wafted through her open window. The tall, skeletal one stood up and, leaning on his hoe, began to smoke a thin brown cigarette, while the one who had acted as spokesman the day before hoisted a bush into his arms. Mrs. Purvis watched the muscles shifting under the skin, as he set the azalea into the earth, and experienced a hot, tingling sensation moving in wave-like ripples through her body. Overwrought by her physical being, she decided to go out at once and remind them they were hired for only one day.

Oh my, a large pile of stones cluttered the driveway, and the third man had begun mixing cement in an old wheel barrel. At first he didn't notice her standing there. She sighed in the damp heat. The pill had been forgotten; and it was now evident there was need for one. When she approached him and inquired about the stones, the other two men joined her. A beautiful wall, just like in the old country. Mr. Purvis felt that she

101

would love the privacy. Oh, dear, the world was shrinking: first the foliage blocking the horizon, now a wall around the house; and Mihal, who had introduced himself as an expert stone mason, assured her that they would not leave until everything was just as Mr. Purvis desired. Oh, well. Lemonade? she offered. They were pleased with her offer and told her directly what a splendid woman she was. How arresting that three strangers thought her splendid! Mr. Purvis, who knew her slightly better, would not agree.

As Mrs. Purvis squeezed the lemons into the icy water, she was thinking about the hand on her arm the day before, and then she recalled a dream she had had just before waking. The man named Mihal was on top of her crushing her with his heavy body and infusing her with his rich botanic breath of lilacs, making her gasp for air; Oh dear, was it really lilacs? She must put the cookies on the tray and go out at once; and as she did, she had a fleeting vision of Mr. Purvis' white body with its folds of overlapping skin. Through the door she went, longing for the first winter snow. If only she lived where the earth was layered in permafrost, she might have been spared all this.

She set the lemonade and cookies on the wrought iron table on the patio and was about to hurry in, when Mihal approached and asked how she liked the section of wall they had just completed.

"I'm very pleased," she replied.

"And next we will seed a most wonderful vegetable garden, which we will care for all through the summer and fall," the man named Jeronim added.

"Vegetables?"

"Yes, Mr. Purvis..."

"Yes, I suppose Mr. Purvis thought I'd like to grow vegetables."

Mrs. Purvis offered the cookies and took one herself. "So where are you from?" she asked, knowingly crossing the line; but, no, that wasn't right. The line had been crossed with the lemonade and cookies. No, no, it was the hand on her arm, the soil dust that had remained and entered her nostrils, becoming a part of her. A connection had been forged. Mihal offered his men cigarettes. They stood around smoking and talking in a foreign tongue.

"We are from Eastern Europe," Mihal said at last.

"Oh," said Mrs. Purvis. So along with the lascivious botanical smells, weed profusions, and the noise and clutter and rattle of lawn equipment, the war, too, was coming upon her. She thought of the silent snow-covered mountains giving way to myriad refugees, loaded with valises and black plastic bags, spreading along the spring slopes and high passes. Without warning the sun assaulted her. She leaned against the table, light-headed and weakened. One of the little pills was in her pocket for emergencies. She withdrew it and swallowed it with a sip of lemonade.

"You are so kind," Jeronim commented, but Mrs. Purvis was lost in thought. "It is Gjergi's birthday today," he continued.

She heard laughter and someone had mentioned a birthday, but she was thinking about her husband now and wondering where he was. After the collapse of the communist regimes he had become infected with the idea that his future lay in the new investment opportunities opening up Eastern Europe and Central Asia. "Telecommunications, computers...any and all consumer products...a desert waiting to be irrigated, I tell you," he had said to a few friends over for drinks one evening, while she sat quietly, as usual, listening helplessly. "Seed money, that's all I need, and I am off and running...coal, gas, oil pipe line materials." He had gotten his seed money in the form of counterfeit 100 bills on one of his so-called high level business trips to Baku. The court had looked upon Mr. Purvis as a dupe and victim rather than a collaborator and cautioned him to stay away from easy money and unstable regimes; but he had been on to something else, even as the warning had been issued. "Something lucrative in Albania, dear," he had told her in a rare intimate moment. And he was off again. Two months later he had returned, sallow and jaundiced, mercurial as ever, one moment speaking in animated tones over the phone, eyebrows raised in curiosity and excitement, the next moment, lying prostrate on the sofa with a drink, taciturn and withdrawn. Then off again and unreachable. And she was slipping again; she could feel it in the hollow echo chamber between her ears.

Dazed, she returned on unsteady feet to the confines of her house, but once there she recalled hearing the word *birthday* and began to bake a cake and prepare her rich, dark blend of coffee. As she mixed the

103

ingredients she wondered about the course she had set for herself. It was as if she were floating downstream on a river that was taking her to a different part of the world. Had it started with the onslaught of spring or at the point of Mr. Purvis' unceremonious departure? Or with the arrival of the gardeners? Somehow she was reconnecting to the world. A shiver made her drop her measuring cup and ask herself whether she wanted to become reconnected. Oh, the summer would bring bulbous purple eggplants, a proliferation of gigantic emerald squash, prickly cucumbers, wild climbing vines of beans, and tomatoes that would crack under the pressure of their juice, releasing potent fruit essences into the air. Could she handle the summer after a spring such as this! And where was Henry?

At four in the afternoon her ruminations were cut short. Shirted and shoeless, the gardeners sat primly on her couch before her pine coffee table and indulged in her cake and coffee, but as the hour wore on, they became less deferential, leaning their oily heads on the back of her sofa and sprawling their legs. Oh dear. I have gone too far, she sighed. As they sipped and chewed, they looked around at the enormity of her living room, which flowed into her dining room; and from there, they could see a porch done in wicker with tufted white cushions; they looked not so much awed as mortified. And then came the statement she had anticipated, a statement to which she could not respond.

"In our country we have three or four families in a place like this; Mr. Purvis is a wonderful man."

She pondered the statement as she sipped her coffee. Was there something she had missed in the remote Mr. Purvis? She had never quite thought of him as wonderful, and the house merely served to emphasise the fact that, though married, they inhabited separate worlds.

"Mr. Purvis must be very wealthy man to help get us here," the tall, gangly one called Gjergi let out, as he gazed about the house.

Mrs. Purvis puzzled over the candor of the remark and wondered if there were anything ironical in it. She searched his face and thought she detected a hint of smirk. Quickly, she rose to clear the dishes, but a hand reached up and touched her arm. "To us, space is the mountains, the sea, the endless forests." The gardener named Jeronim let his hand drop.

"This house..."

"Where do you sleep?" she asked suddenly, curious, fearful.

"In the truck."

"Until Mr. Purvis returns," said Mihal.

Mrs. Purvis' space continued to shrink. Her cheeks felt hot. "And then?"

She thought their demeanors sheepish. She knew what they were thinking, but could Mr. Purvis have intended that? A misunderstanding. He had volunteered to find them a place to stay. During the course of his business a problem had arisen. Someone's relatives, no doubt. The problem had fallen on Purvis, who said *no* to no one but her. When he returned, he would find housing for them. But he had never said when he would return, nor had he telephoned. When she emerged from her thoughts, she noticed that Jeronim had wandered off and was now coming down the stairway into the hall by the front door.

"You won't mind if we ask Mr. Purvis for some of this space?" he said, returning to the living room, ebullient. Forgetting himself, he lit a cigarette and smoked in her house. "We will earn our keep. This will be the most beautiful property." Again she had the impression she was being toyed with. He lowered his voice, addressing Mihal and Gjergi. "Four bathrooms upstairs. Four bathtubs and sinks!" He turned back to Mrs. Purvis, who stood, transfixed with the coffee pot in her hands, staring at the cone of ashes at the tip of the cigarette. "We will cook and clean, tend to everything, inside and outside. Mrs. Purvis, you would like this?"

She looked to Mihal, who sat brooding. And then, seeing Gjergi's frail form and pale skin, she wondered if they were really gardeners at all. And their command of English – thick and slow but somewhat fluent. *A coup d'état*, she observed, considering Jeronim's question merely rhetorical. She walked slowly, weak-kneed and light-headed, into the kitchen, where she leaned over her sink and felt saliva collecting on the walls of her mouth. Mr. Purvis would certainly call tonight, and she would mention what was going on and solicit his advice in the matter of kindly putting these people, who were looking more and more like squatters at every turn, somewhere else. Bracing herself against the sink, she thought of the lemonade and cookies and the cake and coffee and the hand on her arm.

Oh, there had been two different hands soliciting her at different times. Mr. Purvis would ask why she had encouraged all this familiarity.

But Mr. Purvis didn't call, or she had missed the call while napping or stepping out.

The next morning she awoke to the smell of coffee wafting into her bedroom. When she arrived in the kitchen, she sat down to two sunny-side up eggs in a puddle of oil, flecked with what she instantaneously thought of as *burnt offerings*. As she cut into the egg, a plate of coarse biscuits arrived along with her tiny silver bowl brimming with honey. Gjergi made a deep bow and placed it before her.

"Mrs. Purvis, you were asleep when Mr. Purvis phoned; he is detained," Mihal announced, coming in through the kitchen door with earth on his hands. He clapped them together, allowing the dirt to fall on the white linoleum. "Coffee, Gjergi," he said pulling out Mr. Purvis' chair for himself. He pulled out a thin brown cigarette and began to smoke.

She wondered if Mihal meant *detained* with all its various connotations – she was thinking of the counterfeit bills – or did he mean merely *delayed*. Without realizing it, she let out a low guttural moan over such imprecise use of her language. Yes, it was hers and meant to be uttered without the d's and g's confused and the vowels becoming sloshed about as if they were being spit out of a blender. The coffee was strong and bitter, as if the dregs were circulating in the hot liquid as she drank.

"You spoke with Mr. Purvis?" she asked.

Mihal grunted and smoked.

"He always speaks with him. Mr. Purvis did not tell you about us?" Gjergi asked.

Another question that did not beg an answer, Mrs. Purvis mused, as she observed Gjergi's impatience approach agitation. The mouth twitched, then the left eye, the nose; and then the sequence of twitches began anew. He called to Jeronim, and the two sat down at the kitchen table. "It is time to tell Mrs. Purvis," Gjergi said urgently, eyeing Mihal. Oh, the bitter coffee steam swirled inside her nostrils, swelling her sinuses; and her eyes took in the dirt in the men's nails as they picked up their biscuits and slurped their oily coffee. Her throat thickened, as she wondered just what was to assault her sensibilities next. She must call Dr.

106

Mann immediately; it might be time to check into that pleasant little hotel with the pure white square room overlooking the quiet patio.

"Tell her everything," Gjergi urged. "It is time," he continued irascibly, as if tired of the game being played out.

She looked at Jeronim, sitting meekly, eyebrows raised in anticipation. His biscuit and coffee sat untouched and his cigarette was burning down at the edge of his plate. Yes, she thought, they should have just seized the house and its contents straight out! And yes, she was part of the contents, she mused, thinking of Mr. Purvis' pale, fleshy arms that only occasionally reached out to her.

"Mr. Purvis didn't tell you about us," Mihal began. "We knew him in Albania. We saved his life a year ago when Barisha was chased from office. The Albanian people had lost all their money in the pyramid schemes and they were out to get anyone involved. Mr. Purvis, the big American business man..."

Oh, the tone was derisive. These men didn't like Mr. Purvis. It was not what she thought. She heard Mihal's thick voice in the background as she struggled with the thought of her house being invaded. What had Purvis done? She felt blood thickening in her veins. Oh, was her circulation grinding to a halt? Her mind became still and she listened.

"Your husband had no business in our country. He handled dirty money from smuggled goods; he even got hold of Iraqi black market oil." Mihal paused, his cigarette dangling from his lips, which curled into a sneer. "And then he dumped his dirty money into our banks. He went right to the top with his schemes and when the pyramids crashed, they crashed on him and his chum, the president. We found him trampled by an angry mob as he tried to escape. We thought he was just an innocent foreigner caught up in the chaos of our country, but he was one of these men after..."

Oh, dear, so this Mihal was not a gardener or stone mason at all, but an impostor, Mrs. Purvis mused, her throat so tight she thought a fourth man, perhaps a ghost of a man killed in the chaos, was wrapping his gnarled fingers around her neck. A vision of bean vines winding about her neck and binding her arms to her side loomed before her, and she imagined her prostrate body lying in a tangle of prickly overgrown squash plants. Who was he?

"Your silly husband had been dragging an old rusted Kalashnikov, as if he knew how to use it."

"But where would he get one?"

"Twenty American dollars right off the street, like the way you sell umbrellas in the rain."

"Oh, dear." A thin worm slithered out of the muddy earth and disappeared into a squash or into her leg; she wasn't sure. And the red fire ants were on the march over her body. She could feel them devouring her.

"He offered us the world if we saved him," said Mihal, pouring himself more coffee from a small pot on the stove. "So we saved him, not knowing what we saved until it was too late. He was still interested in his grand scams, even as he lay by the side of the road, bruised and feverish." He rose and spat in the sink. "We accepted his offer."

Gjergi was no longer passive. "He got us out and told us we can live in his house," he said, his eyes cast into his coffee cup.

"But where is Mr. Purvis now?"

"He is still busy in Albanian affairs. He is trying to get his money out of *Vefa*, but he won't; and in this respect he is no different than any other Albanian citizen." Mihal stood up, stretched and yawned rudely. "You will be lucky if you see Mr. Purvis again. Albania is not America." He carried his coffee cup to the sink and then walked over to Mrs. Purvis' chair, leaned over her and whispered in her ear. "We will wait here until Purvis returns, whenever that is."

Mihal's breath did not hint of lilacs; it smelled of damp mushroom; and as she inhaled, she felt the spores filling her nostrils and throat. And what if Mr. Purvis does not return, she wondered. Was he desperately trying to find the money to pay off these men? Or had he simply abandoned her – and them? Her eyes closed, but she could feel Mihal's presence, as if his energy field had swallowed hers and she was suffocating. Her rib cage pressed into her lungs and her temples held her head in a vice. She felt that at any minute she might implode, becoming an infinitely dense speck. Oh, she mused, as she struggled for air; she should have seen it all coming with the advent of spring.

As she sat quietly in her chair, she felt two thick fingers at the back of her neck and then she heard a voice. "You won't be in our way if you stay, Mrs. Purvis. You are a good generous woman who married a foolish, greedy man." She felt pressure at the base of her neck. The pressure of the hand was no longer solicitous, as it was during her first encounter; it was now warning her that if she should go to the authorities, something might happen.

She rose from the chair and went out to the back yard, where she stood by the wrought iron table, wondering if the vegetable garden would still be planted and whether the stone wall would remain a work in progress. The air was still and damp. As she studied her yard, it seem to recede from her gaze until it appeared merely a painted canvas and the grass fell away from her feet. Oh, she was becoming detached again. She floated to the kitchen window and peered inside. Gjergi and Jeronim remained at the table drinking coffee and smoking, but Mihal had disappeared. In a moment he returned, dragging a heavy burlap bag, which he hoisted onto the kitchen table. He pulled a knife from his pants and slit the bulging bag open, so that the contents spilled over the table.

Oh dear, Mrs. Purvis mused. Thank goodness she was far away now. She had once worried about being overrun by flowers and vegetables; how silly to worry about spring when the civil strife of a far off country had insinuated itself upon her; but it could not reach her now. She watched the men handling and examining the guns and rifles; they took dish cloths, doused them in her extra virgin olive oil and began cleaning the guns. From her vantage point, they seemed engaged in an elaborate cleansing ritual, probing every nook and cranny of their weaponry, their expressions suggesting deep concentration, their cigarettes dangling from between their lips, forgotten. Suddenly Mihal put down his rifle, drew his cigarette from between his lips and picked up the telephone. Instantly the window thickened, first into a translucent barrier, then an opaque wall, leaving her isolated in an intense damp heat. Oh dear, perhaps Mr. Purvis was finally trying to reach her.

Morag McIntyre Hadley

spent fifty years in trouble for day dreaming before she found writing the daydreams had more street credibility. Her tolerant husband acts as her left brain, most of the time. Somewhat peripatetic, (her clan motto means 'Bundle and Go') has lived in Bangkok, Singapore and England, but now lives in Edinburgh, mainly for the Hills, Haggis and the Edinburgh Festival.

Making History

Morag McIntyre Hadley

I was the twelfth, and last, to be born. So my Mama thought. She'd lost count of how many babies she'd had, how many had died. Mama called me No Name, and fed me on sheep's milk straight from an old ewe's teats. The sheep didn't mind. She'd lost her twin lambs, and enjoyed the heat of the hearth and the warmth of my baby body lying alongside hers.

My Mama sort of lost her mind that bitter winter. Stopped talking, gave up hollering at her brood. 'Cept for me, the last born. She set her little, hard-as-leather feet comfy on sheep fleece and told me the names of her living children. One by one, I caught their names, rolled them round my mouth, then put them in a safe place. For later. I was No Name.

Sometimes, when her mind slid into swamp mud, Mama told me pretty names of babies whose little mouths and cute noses had sunk too deep into the fat, goosedown pillow she'd brought with her from the old country. I sucked and looked up for the voice that was Mama's. Her big hornbill toes wriggled through fleece at happy-telling times and her little, pink-curling toes uncurled themselves and stuck straight out at the bad-telling times.

For the first time in her life, she told me that first winter, she was havin' herself a rest. No infant to feed, and the old man leaving her alone. She reckoned that was on account of their first born being old enough by then for what he wanted.

She was called Donna Notte, a name my mother heard from a

storyteller when she was new married. He was handsome, she recalled. Tall, and singing for his supper, making his way 'cross country to make his fortune. *Donna Notte*, a name to be whispered into the wind, she fancied. I practised running Donna Notte round my little gummy mouth, wondering, I guess, what it would feel like to be called such a thing instead of No Name.

I was No Name. I was a shadow. Later, a bit grown, I slid myself into corners, wound my lanky legs round fat spiders, and dangled from wormed, ham-smoked rafters and watched: looked on as my siblings, well grown, lived out their meagre lives. Mama, I think, forgot to tell them I'd been born. When the old ewe died, I found a place at the end of the long, knotty plank table. No one noticed. No one spoke. I knew my Mama, the others I had to find out about for myself.

Donna Notte, being the eldest, sat right close to Mama. She's small, with hair like maize gone wild, streaming like a mess of stars trawling the skies on a sharp winter's night. Skin, white and cold, like the bowl she fed Mama-without-teeth from. Couldn't see her eyes from where I sat. I wanted to see if the journey of the storyteller, who gave her a name, was in them. I hip-hopped-thumped along the table planks to look.

Her eyes were two sapphire winged humming birds, fluttering the way they do, hovering on the edge of something, waiting to see which way...They stopped fluttering. Suddenly. No journeys in them. No dreams. Not yet. I slithered a way down a nearby leg that shook me off.

Pope Innocent, Pope for short, was Mama's first boy baby. The sweetest she ever did see, she declared, and named on account of a Hell Fire preacher she and the old man had to put up while the preachin' hall was being built.

That preacher, he pounded so hard, and so often, on the arm of the rocker (it being the best chair in the house) he made a smoothed out hollow, near enough the size of an apple. "Pope Innocent!" he pounded. "Pope Innocent! Listen well," he thumped. "Pope Innocent dwells in Hell's everlasting fire. Nev-er for-get his na-me," he walloped. Rock-rock, went the best chair. Creak-creak, went its rockers. Drr-um, drr-um, went the name into Mama's young head.

Brother Pope took the rocker for his own. Summer evenings, he'd haul it onto the stoop and fume into the sunset. Such a special name, such a bonny baby boy. I needed to see his sweetness close to. Easy to place my little foot on the edge of a rocker, loop onto its back and look down on the head of a brother called Pope Innocent.

Silk-sow hair, like barley whiskers, edged a pink globe of bone. Beneath, Pope's hot-coal face glowed in the setting sun's glory. Eyebrows, that should have been Satan black, (I thought) and glowering, were frosted silver. They shimmered over pig-pink eyes. That was Pope Innocent. Pink as a cherub.

I somersaulted down his pot belly. He jerked my head between his knees, pinned me upside down, and glowered at the smothered rose petal sky through the V of my skinny legs. Soon as sun set, his fat knees fell apart and bounced me off into the twilight.

I sprang on to a stripped bone branch of the lightning-hit tree and watched my brothers and sisters gather for the evening. No Name on the branch of the tree that was hit by lightning, on the night of a storm fit to suit Noah. That's what Mama told me.

Mama sits in the middle of the room, watchin' nobody and nothin'. Papa ain't there. Not any more. But the others, they're all there. 'Cept No Name, 'cos I'm out here.

Marie Antoinette, my somewhere-in-the-middle sister, is there. I learned about Marie Antoinette the day my old ewe-milk nanny knew I'd cut my first tooth. She shucked me off, stuck her four legs in the air, causing my hungry mouth to latch on to Mama's big warmed up toe, and bite her good and hard. Mama sort of rolled the name around her mouth. Forgot about her bitten toe. Came out all funny. Not her everyday voice at all – but like it was all the way from France, like Marie Antoinette's name. Here's how.

Once the Hell Fire preacher and his butter-wouldn't-melt wife got themselves settled, Mrs Preacher lady started calling, settin' up quilting parties, and tellin' the women how they should be good, submissive wives. Well, my Mama just up and told that preacher lady, in a huffy-puffy voice that if bein' a submissive wife meant dodging the old man's fist real quick, then she knew already, and Mrs Preacher – she could go an put her pincushion...Mama didn't tell me where.

I was jus' tellin' her this, Mama said, when I noticed her pincushion was the prettiest thing I ever did see. All coloured silk threads, all pretty flowers with loops and leaves. There were hearts and loveknots and half angels, with wings...Mama sighed with remembrance. Preacher lady liked Mama liking her pincushion, an' upped and told her that it had come all the way from Paris, France. It was special, on account of it being a bit of a sleeve from a dress that had belonged to someone called Marie Antoinette.

Mama had to wait a couple of years before she got to use the name, that being the year Giovanni was born. It was worth the waiting. With such a pretty name, coming from a great lady who wore such pretty dresses, Marie Antoinette would be a beauty, Mama said. I wanted to see for myself.

Tall, taller even than Giovanni, and from my tree perch Marie Antoinette is easy to see. Her dress is scarlet. She's pacing round the room like a wild turkey strutting. Her sloeberry, make-sure eyes miss nothing. Crimson swish-swish skirts circling her brothers and sister. Mama-with-no-teeth sits still, crouching in on memories she doesn't know she has. But No Name knows. No Name, the keeper of memories.

Giovanni, he was special. I caught Giovanni's name from Mama one still night when my ewe nurse had a bad dose of wind. My baby ears found her stomach gurglin' soothing. It reminded Mama of flute playing, mouth music, or a Jew's harp – she couldn't quite recall rightaways. So the old ewe obliged and gut-gurgled some more to help jog her memory along.

Turns out, it's way back. Before she got on the boat from the old country. Gypsies, she said. Then said it again because I chortled and squirmed with the sound it made. Gypsies and mandolins. Not flutes, not Jews' harps, but mandolins, and the music of love. Mama's first kiss, smothered in almond blossom, from a young passing gypsy fellow, called Giovanni.

'Giovanni,' my weary, getting-old Mama whispered. Even the old ewe hushed up her rumbling belly to listen to the music of a first love's name. And me, baby No Name, wriggled my toes and cooed.

Quart silver moon's just rising, and the call of a whoop-whoop crane bird drew Giovanni out of doors. Black-clad, named for a first kiss, he's swallowed up by the night. Only No Name could see him. He stretched his long legs down by the water, his beaver brown eyes soft under prima donna lashes. Soft, dreamy eyes, not heeding the snake-slither of No Name from the lightning-hit tree, or my sashaying alongside him, matching his stride, keen-listening for the music that had baptised him. He had the walk of an Emperor, who might dress in emerald silk, a curved sword at his belt. A faint whistle hung on his lips. Giovanni. Alone. No Name swinging 'longside on high, Indian corn.

I leave my handsome brother. Go back to the house. Press my nose against the window pane. Marie Antoinette still striding around, and Donna Notte staring into a far country she don't know about yet. Pope Innocent, rocking, rocking, like he was going to take off somewhere else. Giovanni, a little whistle on his lips, biding in the dark. And little old lady Mama sitting somewhere in the middle.

I miss Mama's voice. Don't think I'm gonna hear it again. But I'm keepin' Mama's secrets safe, the ones she never told, 'cept to me, her last born. I know all their names, their histories, alive and dead. Long days and nights by a fire, an old ewe, and a worn out Mama. That's my history.

A sudden wind helps me up on the roof. Their voices rise through the chimney stack. My eerie cry swoops its way down the chimney and towards the creek so Giovanni can hear.

Mama's old-mad-lady's laughter rings out like new church bells. She can tell No Name's around. I reckon Mama knows what I'm gonna do.

Took myself off to the barn. 'Times, some old, worn out cattle find their way in. They don't mind the shape of me 'longside their bellies. I get warm, get a bit drunk on their smell. It's good. There's bats for company too. This is where I make plans.

First, I got to help Donna Notte. She's afraid of daylight, same as some folk hate the dark. Days when she's got to come out she wears a hat, big as a scarecrow's umbrella, and scuttles like a black beetle to church. Then back. That's all.

Night time is easy to catch her – everyone sleepin', mostly. She sits

115

herself along the stoop rail, hitches up her long, black skirt, and swoops the landscape with darting bird eyes. Searching. 'Course, she don't know what she's searching for. For sure, it's not the old man. Donna Notte knows where he is. So does No Name.

She's there. On the stoop. I slip-slide myself through a slit in the barn wall. Sky's like crushed blueberries and bruised bones turnin' yellow. I whisper a soft, West wind into Donna Notte's perfect ear, up her neat, little nose. I swirl it a little so's it tickles her sweet neck. History words, from a storyteller, long gone, rise and fall with the wind, fillin' her head with things she don't know. West wind whispering, 'Donna Notte'. Storyteller calling, and No Name urging the train whistle to catch the wind. And it does.

'Who-oo, whoo-oo!' Takes only a thistledown puff from No Name to push my sister off the rail, and a bit of help from the wind to blow her 'cross the fields, past Giovanni standing quiet by the water, and down to the west-going train.

Donna Notte, on her way to sun, to sweet growing flowers, and the wide ocean. She's goin' to find her history, a gift from No Name.

The Old Man well dug in under the hog trough, well rotted with hog shit, is our secret. No Name'll keep that safe.

Giovanni, named for a kiss, has music inside him. It's wrapped up in all that blackness, just waitin' to burst out. He's still down by the creek, dipping a black boot in black water. Mooning around. Searching for something.

His velvet eyes, mulberry lips and the sound of hot, gypsy music in his blood were made for passion, not cow herding. I know that passion, he doesn't know he wants, isn't too far away. Next town along is where he'll find it. I'll help him. First, he's got to break a leg.

I'm on the barn roof howlin' like a banshee, like the wildest wolf in the worst ever winter. Even my old, not-so-good-hearing Mama hears it, and they all come running, 'cept Mama.

Giovanni climbs up, and No Name slides down. 'Whee-ee!' Blood curdlin' yell. 'Whee-ee!' Down Giovanni tumbles down the height of the barn. Crunch! And the young doctor rides out from town to save Giovanni and his leg which, he insists, must be healed in town.

The doctor is winsome and gentle. He needs a strong lover who'll look splendid in emerald silk, and who has wild gypsy music in his memory soul. Giovanni needs that young doctor. He don't know it yet, but No Name does.

Marie Antoinette's the family butcher. Spends her days choppin' heads off chickens and trotters off hogs, savaging sweet bunny rabbits with a chopper, and rippin' off cow hide. Smell of blood's like a whore's perfume on her. Poor Marie Antoinette, named for a grand lady from Paris, France.

No Name's mouth craves sweetness for her; I need to hide choppers and knives and tin baths of blood from her, still her wringing hands and rip off those scarlet skirts. Hard to whisper to Marie Antoinette above all that choppin' and heavin' and sploshin'.

She's in the chicken yard. I set myself up on the highest windsail. Arm, leg, arm, leg. One for each sail. No Name spinning, spinning. My spinning brings up the biggest windstorm you ever did see for Marie Antoinette. It sucks up corn chaff from miles around. Marie Antoinette goes on working. I spin some more and spit the wind chaff into my sister's ears. Stuff, stuff. Stuff up her ears so she can't hear chickens squawk, hog squeals and dying cow moans. I spin some more, and flour from the flour bins whips round her, and sticks to her wet, red dress. She spins round and round jus' like a child's top. Her chopper flies from her hand. She's looks like a stick of fairground candy, all twisted red and white. I quit my spinning and windstorm dies. I halt her whirling so that she can hear the silence. She can hear nothing. No screechin' or hollerin' from those poor creatures.

She looks down at her pretty stick-of-candy dress. Starts screamin'
Red on white. Not a pretty dress, not pretty like the sleeve of a dress belongin' to a grand lady from Paris, France. Her screamin', it goes on a long time.

The nuns came, dressed Marie Antoinette in head-to-toe white, placed a pretty circlet of flowers in her hair, and led her away. She'll bake bread – cakes on Feast days. Her knees will turn to cow hide with kneeling, and her eyes become soft and calm with lookin' up at all the angels and cupids. The nuns called her Marie La Blanche. And I'm No Name.

Pope Innocent, a history bearing name, from hell. His fuming and puffing, and fat greasy belly all good for nothin'. He's rocking, as always, watchin' the glory of sunset that's reflected in his pink-pig eyes. Hate, like tornado winds, comin' from him.

I hoist myself up, start see-sawing on Pope's arm. Up and down, up and down. Thumpity-thump, thumpity-thump. Pope doesn't know how come his arm keeps hitting that old rocker. Can't stop it. Like the Hell Fire preacher's, it bangs down and down. No Name see-sawing, I'm having me a great time. Breaking a fat slob arm like Pope Innocent's so easy for me. Crack! Like a snapped stick, and none too clever Pope rampaging like a bull in heat, cursing that Hell Fire preacher, thinking the preacher's thumping caused his broken arm.

I helped him on his way. Up-ended the rocker and catapulted my brother Pope through the air, settin' him right at the door of that old, Hell Fire Preacher.

Pope, he broke the preacher's neck. Law caught him. He'll end up in Hell, 'longside his namesake. Mama's beautiful baby boy in Hell.

. . .

I'll have me that old rocker for my no-teeth, no-memory Mama. We'll set ourselves down by the fire, just us two. No Name, with no history, is goin' to lay her head on her Mama's knee and tell her stories. Just us two, with a not-so-old sheep at our feet when nights grow cold. Mama and No Name.

Celia Bryce

has three claims to fame

— as Julie Walters' double in *The Dancer*.

— her mother doesn't keep asking when I'm going to

get a proper job

— she's possibly the only person in the world to believe

that nursing is a well paid career, now that she's given

it up to write.

Skate Blades

Celia Bryce

I was kind of taken by the man down by the lake. He was new. He was different, I suppose. And I was only, how old? Ten, maybe and the unhappiest boy there ever was.

There was no point in asking Pa about the man. All he ever did was lie in bed now. Didn't see me when he was sleeping. Didn't see me when he was awake. I supposed he wouldn't know much about the man anyway.

And Ma. She wouldn't know either, spending all her time looking after Pa and me, and cooking, cleaning. It seemed no use in bothering her.

He lived closer than anyone I knew, the man down by the lake. That made him our neighbour. And as Ma said being neighbourly was a Christian thing to do, I figured I should go and meet him. She would be pleased with me, thinking about it all by myself. Being neighbourly. She was always having to tell me things. To get washed up for supper. To wake Pa. Find his pipe. Be quiet, when Pa was asleep. Be quiet, when he was awake. And besides, I wanted my skate blades sharpened. That's the one thing we all knew about him. He was a skate grinder.

When I knocked on his door there was no answer, but he was inside. There was every kind of noise coming from that hut. I guessed having knocked twice, it would be OK to just go in there and say hello. Show him my skate blades.

'God damn it! Who are you?'

The man was working in the corner, fixing some hide and soon as I opened the door he dropped the hide on the floor. I watched it fall and how the dust blew up as it landed. I'd never seen so much dust.

'My name's Matthew-John, Sir.'

'Your Ma taught you manners yet?' He stood up big as the roof. Bigger even, bowing his head a little to look down at me.

'Yessir. She taught me to be neighbourly. To new folk.'

'Neighbourly.'

'Yessir. I did knock, Sir. Twice, matter of fact.'

There was everything exciting about the hut. All dirt and dust. Hardly any light at all. It was nothing like my home. Ma made sure of that. Saying cleanliness was next to godliness. I guessed she'd think the devil lived here.

'Well,' the man picked up the piece of hide, 'you've been neighbourly enough for one day. How about you go home now. I got work to do,' he looked hard at me, 'matter of fact.'

Now I wasn't planning on leaving until he'd seen my skate blades, blunt as could be. Needing fixing. And maybe thinking that was the only way he'd get rid of me he fixed them there and then. Made them straight. Balanced a dime on them just to prove how straight they were.

I was watching while he fixed them, then got kind of bored just watching, when all around me were things I'd never seen before. Things I could touch. Pieces of hide and metal, boots hanging from hooks in the wall. Bits of boots – not put together yet. It was a small, dusky place, as if the sun never managed to get in there. But in the corner where he was working there was a cascade of sparks. As if all the light in the world had collected there. Just to be with him. And I forgot all about home, and Pa, forgot about all the bad things that happened there and for a few minutes I forgot about Ma too.

'He don't worry about washing up,' I told Ma, all excited and chewing on a piece of bread.' And when he's sharpening the blades the sparks just fall on the floor – bright as shooting stars. Light the whole place up.'

Ma didn't seem impressed.

'I don't recall giving you permission to go and visit Mr – '

'don't know his name, but on the floor – I didn't see nothing to sweep up with – there's all kinds of things. He makes boots and skate blades and everything. He said I could visit anytime.

I go visiting him almost everyday. Being neighbourly and getting under his hair, I guess, but to me this was the finest place a boy could be. A boy of ten whose Pa wasn't the Pa he used to be and never would be again.

Besides, I figured having me about the place, picking up anything the man dropped and handing it back, asking questions, learning things, would be a good help. And Ma would be proud at least, that I was learning things.

'Now, I guess it's time you were going,' the man said one day. I'd been there most of the afternoon and had every intention of staying forever.

'Ma says I could come any time I choose.' She maybe hadn't said quite that, but I wasn't big on detail.

'Anytime you choose, hey?'

'Yessir.'

'Well, *I* choose, for you to go home now. Got to fix these blades to some boots.'

He was pointing at a pile of new blades, all shining and ready to fix to boots, but I didn't see any straps. You needed straps to fix them, so they were safe to skate on. You wrapped them round your boot and pulled tight. But he wasn't going to use straps. He was going to bolt them on.

'It's better that way,' he explained, 'safer.' He looked down at my feet. Those boots you're wearing, they yours?'

'They're Ma's.'

'You skate in them?'

'Yessir.'

'Your Ma skates in them too, I guess? What about your Pa?'

Did he think all three of us wore the same boots? It was only because Ma's feet and mine were just about the same size, as long as I wore plenty of socks. But Pa?

'He don't skate, I told him, 'he's got no legs.'

I so wanted Ma to meet my new friend. Ludlow was his name. I wanted to share him, I guess. He made me feel so good, and I figured in that green hopeful little mind of mine, he'd make her feel good too.

One day Ma decided to take a walk along to Ludlow's with me. It was the proudest day of my life, taking Ma to visit Ludlow, but it seems Ma wasn't thinking the same way I was.

The hard knock on his door, the way she stood tall and firm until he answered it and the way she looked straight at him made me wonder why she should be angry. Because she surely was.

'Sir.'

'Ma'am'

'May we come in?'

Ludlow looked surprised at Ma wanting to come in. 'I guess so, but it's where I work, so it's not so clean in here.'

'I don't mean to stay long.'

'Coffee?'

'No, please.' She stood inside near the door, still tall and straight. 'Sir, you're putting ideas in to my son's head. It has to stop.'

I looked at Ma then at Ludlow, then at the floor and the ceiling, the dirty little window at the back of the hut and then at Ma and Ludlow.

'And what kind of ideas am I putting in his head, Ma'am?'

'He don't want to go to school, says you never did,' she gave him a look would wither a leaf, 'he don't want to do his school work, his Reader, but he's got to learn.' Ma was wrapping her fingers around her shawl, tying knots in the ends.

'Ma'am won't you sit down?'

'No. Thank you.'

'Ma'am, your son – we – don't talk about school, or Readers, or anything besides skates, and metal, and leather for boots. I don't ask him to come here. He just comes. Likes it here, I guess. But if you want him not to.'

Ma and Ludlow stood staring at each other. Then Ma looked at me and my face burned.

'I have told him not to come. Every night I tell him, and every day he comes here.'

'He sure does,' Ludlow let out a small laugh, but Ma wasn't laughing and Ludlow set his mouth straight again.

'It's not neighbourly to keep turning up at a place.'

'No, Ma'am.'

There was silence. Ma was still twisting her shawl in her fingers, Ludlow was standing his head brushing the roof and I was watching the hem on Ma's skirt.

'Ma'am, would you please sit down. I wiped the chair,' he pushed it forward. Ma she sat down. Ludlow scratched his head. Now that he'd made her sit down in his hut it seemed he didn't know what to do next. 'Ma'am, your son could use some boots, they're wearing thin. He could break an ankle in them.'

'They'll do him till he grows.' Ma was staring down at her hands like they weren't her own.

'You skate too. The boy told me.'

'That boy has not learned when to hold his tongue.'

'He told me how you used to skate with his Pa.'

I looked at Ma's face. Ludlow maybe shouldn't have mentioned Pa. Maybe I shouldn't have mentioned Pa.

'He's a sick man, sir.'

'I'm sorry to hear that, Ma'am. Mighty sorry to hear that.'

I was watching the dust floating on top of the light from Ludlow's stove and wondering if Ma would mention Cleanliness and Godliness, hoping she wouldn't. Hoping that the hot cup of coffee now in her hands, which were clasped tight around it might make her a little less angry with Ludlow. I couldn't tell. But in the half light of the hut I watched the steam rise between them, Ma sitting on the chair, Ludlow on the edge of the table. And the steam was like a soft curtain, something pretty up at a window, letting the sun fall through softly. It was like something Ma might have made once.

Some nights I didn't sleep so well. Those nights I tried to, but somehow always got to thinking that maybe Ma might need me to help her, now that Pa was so sick.

That same night, after we'd come back from Ludlow's was one of those times when I didn't sleep.

'You coming, honey?' Pa's voice was deep. Gruff. With lying in bed all day and night it seemed it just got more gruff. Like how I imagined a bear's voice might be.

'I'll read awhile.'

'Bible reading?'

'I like the bible. Fine stories. Good for our son to know.' Ma's voice was sweet and low. A delicate thing.

I lay in my own bed, huddled up, stuffing my ears with my fingers 'til they hurt but still hearing everything.

'Come here, sweetness,' Pa's voice cut through, sharp like a knife...

'Think of the boy, can't you? What if he wakes?'

'And you think of me.'

Pa scraping his gun off the floor made another noise I couldn't block out.

I didn't want to go to school next morning. Pretended to be sick. But Ma knew a sick child from a well one.

'Get your school books, Matthew-John.'

'Ma, I don't feel so good.'

'I said, your school books. When you're too old for book learning, you'll be wishing you weren't – now, I'll walk with you.'

'To school?'

'Some of the way, yes. See you get there. Don't want you coming back saying some bear tried to eat you,' she pushed her hands through my hair.

It was snowing and I ran on ahead catching the snow in my mouth. Laughing at the way those big flakes landed on my nose.

'You find it funny walking in this weather?'

'It's good to catch the snow flakes on my tongue.'

'You keep that tongue where it belongs. It'll freeze and break off. And then what would you do for talking?

'Tongues don't freeze – only hands. And feet.'

Ma put her arm around my shoulders and hugged me close. 'You're right. It was silly of me to think that way. Look I'm catching them too. Watch me.'

'And me. Look at me,' and I was busy catching snow flakes and watching Ma catch snow flakes but somehow wondering about things at the same time. 'Ma?'

'Yes, son'

'Is Pa going to get better soon?'

She stopped and looked at me, took a deep breath.

'His legs won't grow again, if that's what you mean. Come on we'll be late for school,' she marched on ahead of me.

'Says he's going to make new ones, ' I said, breathless, trying to keep up with her, trying to make her listen, 'wood ones. He's going to make wood ones when he learns how to get out of bed.'

Ma stopped at the top of the hill.

'Let's just wait and see. Meanwhile the school house is that way.'

'Do I have to, Ma?'

'You know so. Now come here, let me kiss you.' I shrugged my shoulders away from her but she caught me up in her arms. 'There's no one on this earth refusing to kiss his Ma, on a day like today. Now. School.'

I did not get to school on time, though I intended to. I wriggled like pup out of her arms and raced towards school, but she hadn't waved at me and I hadn't waved at her and now she was gone, running down to the lake-side, to where Ludlow lived.

'These new blades,' Ludlow was telling Ma, 'I need to test them. If they're good I could make my fortune.'

'My son thinks they'll collapse soon as touch the ice. On account of there being no straps to keep them on.'

'Your son is mistaken, Ma'am.'

She smiled at him and it made her face so pretty from where I was hiding. I wished she'd smile forever.

'Well, I guess now I'm here I could try them for you.'

And I watched Ma pull on the boots and look at them all curious. My heart beating wild in my chest. I had to stop myself running from behind the tree to watch her. Hoping she wouldn't fall on these new, bolted on blades, which didn't look fit to hold up a bird. And yet she stayed upright. On those blades. Thin as knives. Bolted on. And she skated away into the distance. So far, that her face was just a clean white oval. All I could see were her eyes and her mouth. Smiling. Smiling like I'd never seen before. Or else, I never remembered.

'How are they?' Ludlow shouted over at her as she sped around the ice.

'They're fine,' she called over her shoulder, 'fine. Grip real good. Very light.'

'That's the thing. Light. And those strap on blades, a thing of the past, lady. A thing of the past. Safer with bolts. Ludlow's skates – famous whole world over, you'll see.'

Ma swerved around the ice and came back, skidding to a stop in front of Ludlow. And the smile never left her face, reached way up to her eyes and beyond. I figured her golden hair would be smiling too.

'Do you have another name, besides Ludlow?' she asked him, her breath coming out in gasps as if she'd run for miles.

'Guess not. Guess they just called me Ludlow and left it at that. My folks weren't much for words.' Ludlow was looking closely at her. 'Ma'am, may I ask you something?'

'They fit fine. I think these boots, these bolt on blades, will be a success. Truly I do.'

'I know they fit,' he was looking at her closely and raised his hand slightly, towards her cheek. I shook my head, willing him not to, willing Ma not to let him, but it was going to happen and my heart pounded and the wind blew icy in my eyes.

'Ma'am, where'd you get such a bruise on your face?'

I didn't want him to be a party to it, not when she was looking like a whole person again, in those new boots with bolt on blades. But Ludlow found that out, just looking at the mark on her face. And it was as if everything I had hoped for, had gone in that instant.

And what was it I hoped for? Lord knows. But hiding behind that tree, watching Ma and Ludlow, his big hand on her cheek and her whisking away, like lightning across the ice, like she didn't want any part of another man's hand on her face, I knew I was hoping for something and that now it was never going to happen.

It was late and I began making my way back up to the school house. But my legs were heavy and tired with trying to get there quickly and the snow was deep and held me back until I cried with frustration.

The day Ludlow gave me my very own pair of boots, bolt on blades and all, was the day I had my first real fight with Ma. She made me take them back the very minute I got them, or so it seemed. And I was so proud of them, figuring I could be as good as Ma on the ice. As good as Pa used to be. It hurt pretty bad taking those boots back.

The next day Ludlow showed up at our door, carrying the self-same boots. Ma wouldn't let him in, closing the door behind her, so the cold wouldn't get to Pa.

'I'm returning these skates, Ma'am,' Ludlow held them out to her. She shook her head.

'No call to do that, sir'

'I gave them to your son.'

'And I haven't the money to pay for them.'

'Ma,' I tugged at her arm. Ma swung round and pushed my hand away.

'Beg pardon, Ma'am, but they aren't for sale,.they're a gift.'

'A gift, Ma. That sure is neighbourly.'

'Just because my husband is sick, don't mean we need charity.'

'The boy don't seem to mind.' I nodded my head, agreeing with Ludlow that I didn't mind one little bit. He went on, 'charity's a good thing. You read enough Bible to know that Ma'am. The boy tells me you know every page there is. Take them Ma'am'.

'I'll take them, Sir.'

'Matthew-John, I'll thank you not to interrupt! Sir, Ludlow, I can quote any passage from the Bible, that's true. That's why I know there is nothing about giving out skate boots.' Ma's voice seemed full of trembles and I looked at her eyes to see them full of trembles too. Ludlow took her arm and she let out a yelp as if he'd stuck a knife in it. 'Let go my arm, Sir.'

'I meant no harm, Ma'am, no offence. Did I hurt you? I'm sorry if I hurt you Ma'am.'

And Ma put her hand up to her mouth, looking at the door behind her. She shook her head. I knew what this meant. I knew we had to be quiet. Pa was asleep. Or he was awake. Whichever. We had to be quiet. But

Ludlow didn't understand. And suddenly Ma was crying and the sun went in. It felt too cold to be outside, yet neither Ma nor Ludlow showed any inclination to move. I stood beside them, thinking that maybe things would change. If I just waited. That Ma would let me have the boots after all. If only I was patient. And I watched as the shadows collected. And they stuck to the bones of Ludlow's face and to the bones of Ma's too.

'What in the Lord's name is going on in this house?'

'I told him to work. As you weren't here. Had to get out of my bed and sit here, while he did so.' Pa was sitting pointing his gun at me. He'd climbed out of bed onto a chair asking where Ma had gone, asking why she hadn't come back before now and me having no answers, but to say she might have gone to see Ludlow on account of my new skate boots.

'It is – gratifying to see you sitting in a chair, indeed it is,' Ma told him, 'but this is the not way to get your son to work. By frightening him half to death. There is no need for a gun. Besides, I needed to go out. And now I'm back. I will see to his reading. Put the gun away.'

'Is that all you have to say, woman?'

Ma ignored him, shoving off her shawl and hanging it on the nail by the door.

'Matthew-John. It's time to eat. Put down your book and get some bread for me. If you please.'

I looked at Pa, unsure about what to do. Ma looked at me.

'He already ate,' Pa said, 'isn't that so, Matthew-John?'

'Yes, Pa.' And he pointed the gun at me and made me tell Ma all about what I'd eaten. Broth. Bread.

'Leave him be, why don't you?' Ma took my hand in hers.

'Now, you take your Reader, Matthew-John and read it good and hard. You hear me?'

'Yes, Sir'

'Good and hard. And be like your Ma. Good at things'.

And I read. Good and hard. Tried to block out the words I heard. Tried to block out the noise and standing, curious, at my door, the sight of Ma curled up in a ball on the bed. Tried to block it all out, holding my breath until I could hold it no longer and the piss drained out of me onto the floor.

I climbed back into my cold bed and waited.

It was black night. About ten o clock, maybe, but still Ludlow was working. If he was surprised to see me he didn't show it. A small boy going out, dead of night. Time of year when bears wake up, hungry. Didn't even have a lamp with me.

'What is it, boy?' Ludlow hurried me into his hut and closed out the night, bolting the door.

'Nothing.' I felt his eyes on me, but I moved to the stove, sat down by it and warmed my hands which would not stop shaking.

'Everything OK?'

I nodded and fingered a small pile of wood, there to feed the fire. Fingered it until it splintered, until a sharp sliver stuck my finger and made me squeak in pain and while Ludlow tried to remove it I began to cry. Cried until the splinter was out and thrown in the fire. Cried until Ludlow took me on his knee and held me into the rough cloth of his coat. Cried as he smoothed down my hair, stroked my head.

And all the while I tried hard to remember how things used to be, tried to tell Ludlow. But could only remember about Pa getting lost in the blizzard and being brought home. Half dead. Knew he was only half dead because that's what folks said when they carried him in frozen. But his feet were dead. Burnt by the cold. Burnt so they had to come off.

I stood up and poked a stick into the front of the stove. Ludlow lifted the lid and let me poke about in there, too. Bright red sparks shot out. I watched them rise to the roof, thinking how they looked like fire flies shooting out of nowhere into a black sky.

Then I remembered all the things I had forgotten. Remembered taking walks in the sun. Taking walks in the evening. Running and tumbling with Pa. And hunting. I so loved hunting with Pa, knowing his words off by heart, *you be still now, boy. You spook him and we starve, d'you hear?* The prey could have been small as a hare. Big as a bear. Bigger. And that hard light in Pa's eye as he aimed to shoot. When I saw that light I just knew to keep still, not move a hair, not blink an eye, because if I did the prey was gone. Bolted. And the surprise, some days, when Pa just let an animal go. Stared it down, paralyzed it until he could have taken his shot.

131

And then he just let it go. The power of it. That he could do that and still come home smiling and proud as a man that killed bears all day long.

The red hot sparks disappeared and I watched until the very last one spiralled to the roof and the stove lid was dropped into place. I stopped crying and talking, just sat close into Ludlow's chest. Listening to the long deep breaths he was taking, listening to my own shuddery little breaths, feeling the warmth there was from Ludlow and the stove, with me squeezed in between.

'Maybe' maybe your Pa hasn't got used to having no legs. Maybe when he does, he'll feel better.'

I nodded my head slowly, knowing that Pa would never get used to having no legs.

'Ma says God is good, saving him like he did.'

'If that's what your Ma says, then she's right.'

I looked at my own feet. At my boots. At Ludlow's boots. His legs. Wondering, how is God good when everybody else has feet and Pa had none?

'You tired? Maybe I should take you home now?'

But I did not feel like going home just yet. Said I wasn't a bit tired and just laid my head on Ludlow's big shoulder to watch the fire burn in the stove.

Ludlow was outside chopping wood when I woke. I rose and watched him sleepily from the doorway. Watched the big man heave the axe over his shoulder and bring it down onto the heavy log. I saw the white insides of wood gleam under the sun and where the wood chips fell I was surprised to see how wet the snow looked. I guess spring had come.

I knew that Ludlow would be leaving soon, to find himself new work for the summer. In the city perhaps. I hadn't seen him for days. I went to the door. It was locked. Sometimes I heard him working inside, but Ludlow gave no answer when I called his name, or knocked on the door.

But with the snow disappearing there were new things to do. People to see. My friends ran around like they'd been hidden under a rock for the winter. Ma brushed the floor with the door open, letting the good spring air tumble in.

Sometimes she even hummed to herself. Pa's hair was cut, his beard shaved. He looked cleaner. Brighter.

One fine morning Ludlow came to the door with an invention. Somebody else's invention, he said. I ran inside. Shouting that Ludlow had come. Ma smiled up at Ludlow and then stopped, her eyes fixed on the contraption.

'What in the world is that?'

'It's an invention, Ma!' I was running around looking at every shining bit of it and the smoothed-down wood which gleamed.

'It's for your husband. I figured he might use it.'

'Can I show Pa?'

And all the while, as I tried to push and pull that contraption through the doorway pictures were tumbling about my head. Big, bright pictures, filled with sunshine, so much sunshine they made my eyes squeeze up. There I was, like a big man, pushing Pa in the chair across the grass and the ruts left by the frost, pushing so hard and so fast, Pa laughing and begging me to slow down, or else he would surely fall like a pile of wet wood. And Ma. She was there too, running behind, panting and laughing, begging me to slow down so she could catch up.

'Look, Pa. Look what Ludlow made. It's for you, Pa. He invented it.'

Ludlow and Ma stood in the doorway. I looked from one to the other. Ma, Pa and Ludlow. All with mouths set in line. I jumped into the chair and it ran away with me, hitting the table. Ma let out a laugh. It was like a small piece of glass breaking. Ludlow turned to go.

'Wait up, Sir.'

And I saw Pa's face, dark with something I couldn't understand. It frightened me more than anything I'd seen before. He picked up his gun.

'Didn't I say I was making wood legs? Didn't I, boy?'

'Yes sir.'

'And what am I going to do with those wood legs? Lie 'em up against the wall and look at them?'

'No, Sir. You gonna walk in them.'

'You got it, son. Right on the nail. Don't need no chair with wheels. Ain't even straight wheels.'

I looked at the wheels, they were not straight. They were kind of

133

crooked. I watched him raise the gun to his shoulder, aim it at the chair which stood stock still on its wheels. Stock still under his eye, his hands which were strong and steady, which could kill a bear with just one shot.

'Don't Pa, don't.'

Ludlow moved in front of Ma and made to pull me out of the way. But I shrugged him off, ready to cry.

And then my head cleared. I knew not to move. Just knew it. Moving spooked things, made them run. Pa's words raced round my head. *You be still now, boy.* And I was still, not moving a hair. Not blinking, just watching. *You spook him and we starve, d'you hear?*

The prey could have been small as a hare. Big as a bear. Bigger. And that hard light in Pa's eye as he aimed to shoot. When I saw that light I just knew to keep still, not move a hair, not blink an eye, because if I did the prey was gone. Bolted.

Sylvia Baker

Lives in Dorset, but holidays in Ireland have provided much of the material for her writing – particularly the pubs and lochs and especially Sheeh's Bar in Skibbereen where a certain gentleman named Jerry inspired a character in both her last novel and the short story in this anthology! She plans to end her days lazing by those lochs and boozing in those bars – and of course writing.

History of a Vagrant

Sylvia Baker

I never had the courage to swim in the lough. I'd stand with my brothers on the quay, my toes gripping the edge of the warm concrete, my eyes fixed on the waves shimmering in the distance. But all I could think of was the terrifying depth of the water. The black cold depth of it. One-by-one my brothers would dive in, disappear. And I'd wait for their heads to break the surface. Watch as they pushed soaking hair from their eyes and pinched the snot from their nostrils. But I never had the courage to join them.

I haven't seen a single one of them since I left home. But I see them in my dreams. They're blue with cold, spraying water as they rise together like playful dolphins. Bernadette is with them, floating on her back, the sun on her face. But when my brothers come swimming to the quay, the drops of water on their shoulders sparkling like diamonds, Bernadette still floats there. Her body tossed on the swell. And I can see that her eyes are wide open, her lips parted.

But it didn't happen like that. It's just my conscience giving me bad dreams. She could swim like a fish. Half a mile across the lough would have been nothing to her. She was fooling around; punishing me for going. The way that girls do.

Since I've been in England I haven't had much to do with girls. I see plenty of them, hundreds every day in the passing crowds. Mostly their legs. It's like a moving forest of them hurrying by. When a coin clinks down beside me, I look up and say, God bless you. They don't expect that, and it makes them smile. And sometimes Bernadette's black eyes are in the smile. Then she'll follow me for the rest of the day, dancing in front of me on hot pavements, arms out to stop me passing. Like she used to. And I want to cut the memory of her from my brain. Take a knife and slice it away. But I haven't the courage for self-mutilation. I haven't a drop of courage in my whole body.

I moved to a new place last week. It's a worse dump than the last one. Doors ripped off and the floors and walls stained with filth and graffiti. But I sorted myself out a little corner. That's all I need these days. And then this morning someone tells me it's due to be demolished. It keeps happening to me; this is the third time in a row. So I'm beginning to wonder if it might be an omen. Fate telling me to go home. Well, if they pull this place down, I'll go. I really will go home. I'll either close my eyes while the plaster and the bricks and the slates off the roof come crashing down to bury me – or I'll go home.

On my last night at home all I wanted to do was get away. But I had the farewell gathering to cope with first.

We got to O'Malley's early. My mother liked to sit where she could see who came in, and you didn't get much choice if you left it too late on a Thursday – Gerry's night. By nine o'clock all the seats were filled and it was standing room only for late-comers. I wedged myself in between the bar and the piano, longing for Gerry to arrive so there'd be no more well-wishing and enquiries about where I was going and what job I'd be doing over in England. And every time the door swung open, letting in a rush of damp night air, I thought of the lough and how the tide would soon be changing. The water heaving itself round in the darkness. And the terrible way it roars out into the Atlantic Ocean. Millions of gallons forced through that narrow channel.

And there was Gerry pushing his way through the door, holding it for his partner with the big black mandolin case. The measured smile and his hand raised to the welcoming cheer.

I took him his Guinness as I always did, setting it down carefully on top of the upright piano. He winked at me, arranged his packet of Silk Cut and lighter next to the glass, and settled himself on the stool. The lid of the piano was already open, the worn keys waiting for the magic of his fingers. He took a couple of sips of Guinness, wiped the froth from his lips and he was away. Just a few chords at first so Billy could tune in on his mandolin.

Gerry's voice is made for the songs he sings. Tales of love and death and patriotism. Its tenderness, raspy from too much smoking, can silence a roomful of drinkers in seconds. But he only ever sings a couple of opening numbers, then he stops. He'll light another Silk Cut, take a few dainty drags, start on his second Guinness maybe. Taking his time before he swivels round on the stool. Letting us know that it's our turn.

On my last night there were tourists – there usually is through the summer – and they often request songs. They'll call out the name of it, and then Gerry will cast his eyes round the bar. Playing the first few notes to coax out a singer. And someone will stand up, usually protesting a little, 'Oh, I've got a sore throat this evening' or 'You can't be wanting this old thing again'. But they always sing in the end.

I watched while my Auntie Kathleen got to her feet, adjusting the neck of her low-cut dress, patting the sides of her swept-up hair. She would call me up with her. She always did when people asked for 'Pal of my Cradle Days'. And how the hell would I be able to sing with Bernadette floating out to sea like a piece of driftwood? But it was expected. Then everyone would wish me luck and make a collection for me. My brother got nearly a hundred pounds when he left.

It was through him that I met Bernadette. I took over his weekend job cleaning the holiday chalets at Baltimore. Bernadette was supposed to show me the ropes but I wasn't going to be told what to do by a sixteen-year-old schoolgirl, so I got on with things my own way. But she was laughing at me round doorways; leaning over my shoulder as I scrubbed the grease from cooker tops; stretching herself out like a cat on the flower-patterned duvets. Whatever room I was working in, she was there. Checking on me, she said, because boys didn't know the first thing about cleaning. Sometimes she had her black hair in a plait, the way she wore it for school. And sometimes she'd sit on the bed and unravel it, combing it through with her fingers. And she'd put on lipstick, boasting to me how she'd stolen it in Skibbereen. And one day she painted a stripe down my cheek before I could stop her.

I got Auntie Kathleen's lipstick all over me that last night at O'Malley's. She was bobbing down to kiss me and pull at me, trying to get me out of my seat, her freckled breasts bulging out of her Thursday night dress.

'Come on now, Michael,' she was saying. 'A last duet with me.'

Gerry was watching us over the brim of his glass, his cigarette between his fingers, the spiral of smoke turning the Guinness to brimstone. And my mother was urging me to get up, too. Elbowing me in the ribs. She couldn't sing anymore; smoking and bronchitis had wrecked her lungs and stolen her voice.

'What's the matter with you, Michael?' she said. 'It's your last chance. It'll be unlucky for you if you don't sing.'

Christ, Jesus, unlucky! I thought, while an invisible fist twisted itself in my guts. Heads were turning now, a blur of faces and all the mouths opening and closing, chanting at me to sing. And Gerry's fingers already tripping over the keys, coaxing out those sweet notes.

I don't know how I got through it. Everyone watching me. My mother's eyes fixed on me. She was smiling at me through the haze of smoke, and I was thinking, she'll be coughing all night; coughing and crying because she'd be on her own from now on.

When it was over Gerry pointed a finger at me. 'That was beautiful, Michael,' he said. 'You sang with an ache in your heart.'

'It's leaving you all,' I said.

Billy winked at me and ran his thumb across the strings of his mandolin. 'Well, if things don't work out for you in England, come back and we'll do a recording. We'll be like the Fureys. We'll get rich and famous.'

'You'll be back for Christmas, won't you?' said Gerry. 'You'll be here to sing with us at Christmas.'

'Yeah, sure I will,' I heard myself say. 'Sure I will.'

But summer's here again, and I haven't been back. I'm too scared. They

140

might say I pushed her. I didn't even call my mother for a couple of months. When I did, my brother Liam answered.

'What are you doing back at home?' I asked. He'd moved to Cork after he got married three years ago.

'Damn you to hell, Michael,' he said.

'What's the matter?' I said, feeling like a big stone was in my chest.

'Where have you been? Why haven't you been in touch?'

'Where's Mam?' I said. 'Let me speak to her.'

'You're too late, Michael. You're too fucking late.' The anger dissolved in a sob, and then I knew what he meant.

'When?'

'Ten days ago.'

'Her chest?' I asked, swallowing down my own tears.

'And worry...and fucking worry about you. And she's buried now, Michael. Do you hear me, she's buried?'

And how could I ask about Bernadette? How could I say, have you seen that girl from Baltimore? My mother's dead but I'm asking about that girl from Baltimore. I want to know, is she dead too? But Liam had already put the phone down.

I'd got myself a job in Regent's Park Zoo, chopping up food in the small mammal house, but I didn't feel like going the next day. Just the thought of the terrible stink in the place made me want to throw up.

I went round the florists instead. But I didn't have enough money. The girl had made out the form for Interflora and she got funny when I spread out the coins on the counter and it was one pound fifty short. 'Do you want me to keep the paperwork until you come back?' she said, sarcastic as anything.

'Don't bother,' I said. 'It's too fucking late, anyway.' I never went to work again after that.

We nearly got caught once. Bernadette's uncle came to empty the meter and we were entwined like snakes in a nest. We didn't hear him until he started cursing because he was having trouble with the key. I nearly broke my back trying to get up and out of it. After that we found new places. We couldn't take any more risks; her father would have broke more than my back – killed me probably; she was only just sixteen.

There's a track tucked under the mountain by Lough Ine. It winds up through the woods, past the grotto where a plaster virgin stands beside a pool. People have looped plastic beads round her neck and the blue paint is chipped from her gown, but she still looks so pious that you have to cross yourself as you pass her. But not Bernadette. She'd even wash herself in the pool. She'd crouch down and splash the water up her legs. When I told her she ought not to be doing that, she just laughed and said it would clean away her sins.

That last night we went down by the lough. Bernadette said she wanted to walk. She kept saying she hated the haircut I'd had ready for tomorrow. I wasn't too keen on it myself, but the barber in Skibbereen was stuck in the habit of years. When we were boys it was no good pleading, not too short, Mr Murphy, because our mam had given instructions to get those clippers right up the back of our heads. It was more than he dare do to let us out of the chair with anything less.

I got fed up with Bernadette gibing at me, and I asked was she trying to pick a row on our last evening together? In a way I hoped she was. I'd promised to be back for Gerry's night and there's a limit to how much you can rush a girl – even someone like Bernadette.

'You might not be going to England, after all,' she said, walking on in front of me, hitting out at branches, showering us with drops of water from the trees.

I had no idea what she meant, not an inkling. She liked to talk rubbish if she was in a bad mood. To annoy me. Though I'd a lot to learn about why girls do those sort of things. I even flattered myself it was because she was upset I was going.

We went down by the old quay where I used to watch my brothers swim. Bernadette sat on the edge, her legs dangling above the water. I told her to be careful. I'd never lost my childhood fear. I was brought up on it: fear of my elders and betters, fear of divine retribution, fear of Sister Justine's ruler that'd come smacking down when you least expected it.

'You'll have to marry me,' Bernadette said suddenly, kicking her heels against the concrete.

'Mind your shoes don't fall in the water,' I said.

'Stop worrying about me shoes,' she said. 'We've a bigger worry than them.'

'I'm going to England,' I said.

'No you're not. I'm pregnant.'

All I could think of was that I mustn't be late back, mustn't be late for Gerry's night. And I said what blokes the world over have said in this situation. 'How do you know it's me?'

She jumped up. 'You're a rat, Michael.'

'Well it's not just my fault.' God, she was going to ruin everything. I hadn't even started on living yet and she was going to ruin it.

'Yes it is!' she spat at me. 'You don't pull it out soon enough.'

I turned to walk away and she started crying. 'I'll jump in the water if you don't come and see me dad.'

'Jump,' I said. I didn't mean it, but I didn't know how to deal with her. I could hear the ocean in the distance. Crashing like thunder on the rocks. See the spray rising a hundred feet in the air. But the lough hadn't a ripple. If she did jump – and I didn't think for a second that she would – then she'd be safe enough. The strong fearless girl she was.

'I have to go,' I said. 'I've promised me mam.'

She ran to catch up with me. 'I'm coming with you.'

At that stage we were just two people not wanting the same thing. And when I turned on her, shouted at her to leave me alone and let me think, we were just two people about to have a row. But when she ran back and jumped in the lough, we were two people with our lives changed forever.

I carried on walking. What did she want? Did she want me to jump in after her? All the times I'd whispered, I'd do anything for you, Bernadette, came crowding in my head. All those desperate deep feelings of first love. I ran back. God knows how long I stood looking down into the water, watching the surface break and shift like some monster was waking up beneath it. But there was no sign of her.

And all evening I watched the door at O'Malley's. Watched for her to come through it. Prayed for her to come. Nobody said to me, where's that wild girl from Baltimore you've been seeing? Nobody expected her to be at Gerry's night.

The digger moved in this morning. It took out the front garden in one chunk, slicing up rubbish and earth and broken concrete. They'll start on the house tomorrow. The other squatters have gone. They think I'm crazy staying on here. They don't know about the decision I have to make. That it's driving me mad not knowing.

The sounds of grinding and crushing are getting closer every hour. But I've the courage to stay if I have to. I'll just sit tight with a packet of fags and a few bottles of Guinness. And maybe I'll sing some of Gerry's old songs. And I'll think of home. I'll imagine the noises are the sea, the way it crashes through that narrow channel. And then maybe I'll work up the courage to make that phone call. And if Bernadette's there I'll sing to her down the phone. Maybe she won't have time to listen. Maybe the baby will be crying. And I'll say, fetch him over. And she'll tuck him in the crook of her arm, the pair of them plump and happy the way I know they'll be. Then I really will go home.

Ian Baker

I am a native of the industrial wasteland of Teesside, North East England, an area decimated by the lunatic policies of Thatcherism (although I now live in Ballyconneely, Connemara with my wife and two daughters). As a young man I was an active participant in the Great Punk Wars of 1977 and enjoyed the privilege of not only seeing the Sex Pistols live, but sharing a can of lager with the great Sir John Rotten himself. When I wasn't working packing false limbs into boxes, I was stacking bricks into metal cages to be collected by fork lift trucks. I worked as a builder's labourer and, in between jobs, completed an arts degree.

I am currently working as a salmon farmer and was fortunate enough recently to race with a school of dolphins, (an experience from which I'm still buzzing). I have been writing for about two years and *All the Good Times Too* is my first published piece of writing.

All the Good Times Too

Ian Baker

Standing in the queue, I can hear them sniggering behind me.

"Size of the lugs on that."

More laughter, then shuffling and a slight movement behind. Girls' voices joining in.

"Puff the Magic Dragon, lived by the sea."

"Ah leave him be."

Without warning the queue surges forward and I feel hands on my back. I'm pushed hard and fall against the boy in front who turns round, angrily.

"Watch it!"

The next thing I know Mr Lewis, the headmaster, pulls me out by the collar. Everyone laughing.

"You! What's your name? Stand over here and don't move until I tell you."

She didn't turn up and in the end Miss Carling comes out. All the others have gone and I'm stood at the gate on my own, not sure which way to go or even if I should. Miss Carling gives me a lift in her funny car. I give her the name of my street and she knows it so that's okay. It's called a Citroen. The car that is, not my street. Miss Carling takes me to the door and rings the bell and waits with me. My mam comes to the door and she's wearing a dressing gown. An orange dressing gown.

"Oh," she says.

Playing football in the street. I've got the ball at my feet and I'm trying to find a way past David Rudge and I'm trying not to trip over myself. Someone shouts something but I don't look up or round. I know what it is and I don't want to know. David Rudge steals the ball and goes racing up the street. I look up then. I can't stop myself, even though I know what I'll see. I look at our house and my mam's stood near the curtain, tapping on the window and tapping her ear, signalling to me to tuck my ear in behind my hair.

"You'll be on the right wing, off you go, good luck."

As I walk out onto the pitch I see my dad in amongst the other dads. He waves and gives me the thumbs up. I'm nervous. All those people. All those dads.

The game kicks off and I guard my position like a sentry. I think about what the sports teacher said.

"You'll be on the right wing."

I'm standing there watching as lads run up and down past me, kicking the ball to each other. No-one says anything to me. I must be doing okay. I look to the crowd and see people laughing and pointing. My dad looks angry and he's shouting something and I can't hear him. He's waving his hand about. After a while the sports teacher comes up to me and says,

"Okay, well done,"

He takes me off then, substitutes me. As I walk towards the laughing dads I look for my dad. I see him. He's walking towards the car with his back to me; I call him but he doesn't turn round and I can see him shaking his head.

"If he sits here then I'm moving."

Potatoes, carrots, peas, cabbage, steak and kidney. Chocolate sponge and custard. No empty seats. Late into the dinner-hall. The tray feels heavy and the steam is making my head sweat. Then I spot an empty space. I make my way through the tables.

"Just stood there," someone says.

"Stood still like a frightened rabbit."

More laughter.

I reach the table. It's Alison Southgate's table.

"If he sits here then I'm moving."
I stand rooted to the spot, not knowing what to say. Eventually Stuart Porter says,
"Oh go on, sit down,"
Alison Southgate scowls at me but she doesn't move. Nobody speaks though – not to me. To each other. I throw my carrots and peas and cabbage on the floor when no-one is looking. I spill some custard on my shirt and feel stupid. I feel my face going red and I want to crawl under the table and hide amongst the vegetables and shoes. Alison Southgate speaks then. She says, "it's alright."

I've got him by the hair and I'm banging his head into the wall. He's strong. He's hitting me and it's hurting but I can't let him win. We are stronger than them after all. We are better.

Paul Boatman thinks he's a car. Although not really my best friend, he lets me play with him sometimes. He runs around the playground going,
"Brrrrm, vrrrm, screach, brrrrrm."
I run around beside him. He's the driver and I'm the passenger.
Sometimes when I've nobody to play with I'll listen out for Paul. When I hear his engine revving and his brakes screeching I'll run up to him.
"Give us a lift then,"
"Hop in,"
"Brrrm, vrrrm, screach, brrrrrm."
Paul Boatman smells bad.

I'm not sure where the toilets are and I need a wee really bad. I go behind the huts where no-one can see me and start to wee. Miss Tunstall runs over and grabs me by the hair and slaps me hard.
"You dirty, filthy boy."
She pulls me from behind the hut, out into the playground, in full view of everybody. In full view of Alison Southgate. My zip is down and my tail is still out. She takes me into the class. She gets a ruler and makes me stand still in front of her with my arms by my side.
"Do you know what happens to dirty boys?"

I stand in front of her with my head down. I'm ashamed.

Loud this time.

"I SAID DO YOU KNOW WHAT HAPPENS TO DIRTY BOYS?"

"No miss, sorry miss."

And she hits me on the tail with the ruler and I start crying. But I don't tell anyone.

Bath time. Me and my younger brother, Simon. We share the bath and mam is in washing our hair. Mam starts laughing.

"I think you were at the back of the queue when they were being given out. Not like Simon here. I think Simon got more than his fair share. I think Simon must have got some of yours as well. Maybe God thought you were a little girl."

"A bottle of Gin and a hot bath," she says to me.

"It's just that I was so young and we were barely just married. I wasn't ready. I had my whole life in front of me and then, well, you do understand don't you?

As I run in through the kitchen door, I throw my bag onto the floor. Something smells good. I'm late. They're all eating. Mam turns and smiles at me.

"Ears our Iain."

Everybody laughing at a familiar family joke. I smile at them and then laugh too. I'm hungry.

Every Sunday.

It's Sunday. She's holding my nose and my head is back. She's forcing the cabbage into my mouth and I'm gagging and choking. Dad and Simon sit and watch but they don't say anything. She's screaming at me but I can't help it. It just won't go down and then I'm really sick, all over my plate and the clean table cloth. She starts to slap me round the head and I'm looking at Simon and then at dad. I've got sick on my chin and on my Sunday best.

"I'm sorry, I didn't mean to..."
Dad says, "If only you'd eat your dinners."

Orange on white. Why? It's slapping about on the kitchen floor, mouth opening and closing, and I'm wondering how it got there? Slap. I pick it up and place it back into its bowl and she comes at me, from out of nowhere. She has a fork in her hand and she lunges but she misses because her eyes aren't seeing right and her balance is all over the place. She falls to the floor then, crying, saying something I don't understand. Her words are coming out all thick and half-formed, like they are not coming from her at all but from somewhere else, somewhere far away. Her mouth opening and closing then opening again, forming an 'O'. Her dressing gown's half-open and she's slapping about all over the kitchen floor. Slap. Orange on white.

It's six-thirty in the morning. I'm sat next to dad in the car. He's driving us to work. Dad's the manager of a brickworks and he's got me a job there as a labourer. It's my first day. It's still dark outside. And still. It's cold inside because the car hasn't had time to warm up yet.
"I should've killed her years ago," he says.
I look at my dad and say nothing. My dad never tells me anything so I decide that that's the way I should play it.
"Too late now," he says. "Too late now."

The new boy is stood with his back to the wall. David Rudge and me are taking it in turns to slap him in the face.
Slap.
"Your turn."
Slap.
"Your turn."
Slap.
"Your turn."
Slap.

She's stopped moving but she's still on the kitchen floor, curled up in a ball and moaning. Her knees under her chin like that she looks like a...

I tried to remove it with the curved end of a coat hanger but I was unable. It was too late. It was stuck, half way between the plug-hole and the U-bend. in the end I had to get dad to help and he got his spanner and removed the washer. I was able to get it out then. It was dead of course. Dad shook his head. I wrapped it in a tissue. Orange in white. I put it in a matchbox and buried it in the back garden.

I remember one time at school. Or maybe it was at home? Anyway, the sky went black in the middle of the day and there was a hailstorm. The hailstones were as big as golf balls and they were crashing into and bouncing off the windows. We thought the windows would break. I was really scared and Miss Carling, or was it my mam?, whoever it was anyway put their arm around me and held me until the storm stopped. We went outside then and collected as many golf ball sized hailstones as we could carry. It took them ages to melt.

I'm in a class of one. The only one in the class. Everyone else is on the school trip. They've gone to Holland.

"I've never even been abroad so I don't see why you should go,"

So I'm sat at my desk drinking my milk and Miss Atkinson is wondering what to do.
"This has never happened before Iain. I don't really know? I'll have a word with Mr Lewis and see what we can come up with. Wait here and drink your milk, I shan't be long."
I'm hoping that I might get sent home, but when Miss Atkinson returns she takes me into a class with the second years.
"This is probably the best idea, Iain."
The first and second years didn't go on the school trip as they were still a bit too young. The trip was for the third and fourth years. Alison Southgate was on the trip. And Paul Boatman. Paul Boatman is scruffy and poor. He has seven brothers and a sister and sometimes he wears odd shoes for

school. And he smells. We're not poor and I only have one brother and my shoes get polished every morning.

Everybody is excited, talking all about the trip. Paul Boatman has got himself a bigger engine. Now it goes 'zoom' instead of 'brrmm.' Alison Southgate and Stuart Porter are going out with each other. Holiday romance. Everybody gives presents to the teachers and then they show each other photographs. The whole lesson is about Holland and the teacher asks the class about Holland and what they did there. She doesn't ask me about Holland. I think it's all dead boring anyway. I tell them that we did 'The Lion, The Witch And The Wardrobe.'
"We did that in first year," says Elizabeth Sharpe.

Afterwards I feel guilty and when I see that David Rudge is playing football in the school field, I find the new boy and I say sorry to him and make friends. He's called Adrian. He's really nice and he invites me to his house for tea where we play with his 'Thunderbird' toys. His mam and dad are really nice too.

Afterwards, when I wake up, I feel awful and I'm sick into a bucket at the side of the bed.

Afterwards, when I wake up, I feel a little better. I'm on the school field and David Rudge is beside me.
"You've been asleep for ages," he says.
We walk back to our street and when I get to my house he wishes me good luck.
"Thanks," I say.
I tell mam and dad that, yes, I did go to 'The Electric Onion', but that I wasn't drinking and that some lad next to me had got drunk and was sick all over me. Dad is furious but mam is laughing.
"Is that why you've got sick running out of your nose?" she says.

When I've stopped being sick the nurse wipes my mouth for me and asks me how I feel.

"A bit groggy," I say.

I feel the big bandage on my head. My head is sore, my ears hurt a lot.

I've still got sick on my chin and in my dinner. In my cabbage and on my shirt.

"I suppose he'll have to leave it now," says dad.

My stomach hurts from being sick.

Carrots, peas and cabbage on the floor under the school dinner table and custard on my shirt and my stomach hurts because she spoke to me. It feels like I've just been punched.

"It's alright."

My stomach hurts where he's been hitting me. I stop banging his head against the wall and we separate and circle each other.

"Do you want some more?" I ask him.

"No," he says, "no more."

"Well fuck off then you black bastard,"

Dad and me spent ages making it. It was a mock-up of the surface of the moon, complete with landing craft. It was made out of papier-mâché and toilet rolls and cereal boxes and bits of cardboard. Every night we'd be at it, after school and after dad finished work. Hours. It looked fantastic when it was finished. It was for the open-day at the cubs' hall. There were prizes to be given out for the best display as well. I was sure I'd win.

On the big day dad and me went along to the cubs' hall, looking at all the displays on all the tables. I was tingling with anticipation and pride. We couldn't find it. We looked again, up and down the rows, looking at all the tables. It wasn't there. My dad said something to the scoutmaster and they went and had a look in a cupboard in the hall and there it was right at the back of the cupboard, covered in dust. They'd forgot to put it out. It was too late to do anything about it then, so he gave me a Mars bar.

"I wonder what your future wife will think when she sees that?"

I have this ugly brown birth-mark, on my hip. It really bothers my mam.
"You could get cancer from that, if you're not careful."
The next time after swimming, I find that I'm covering myself up with my towel in the changing rooms. It never used to bother me before.
"Some women might not like it."

Dad picks me up from the hospital and takes me home in the car. When I get home mam starts laughing and tells me that I look like "a Paki" with my bandages on.

The selotape feels really uncomfortable but mam won't let me take it off. When I do finally get to remove it it stings when it takes some of my hair out with it. She inspects my ears.
"No different," she says.

I can hear crying downstairs. It sounds odd. Wrong somehow. My brother, Simon, comes out of his room, rubbing at his eyes.
"Go back to bed," I tell him.
I creep down the stairs and into the living room. Dad is sat in the chair with his face down in his hands.
"Dad?" I say.
Dad looks up and tries to smile but he can't. He looks embarrassed. He gets up and puts his arm around me.
"It's okay." he says.
I don't know what to do.
"Where's mam?" I ask.
"Come on, it's late. Back to bed with you."
I look at the clock and see that it's four-thirty in the morning. Mam hadn't come home from work yet.

She's wearing big bunny ears and a fluffy tail. I think she looks very pretty.
"Don't I look pretty?"
"The prettiest mam in the world."

Tjinder was his name. He was from India. He'd only been at the school a week. I went to his house for tea and I had to take my shoes off. His mam and his dad and his sister were all very nice. His dad was a doctor. The food was different from what I was used to at home. We sat on the floor on cushions and they put on this strange music, and afterwards we sat and talked and they asked me all about myself and then they told me all about India. I had a good time. Another time, I brought him back to our house for tea and mam and dad were very polite to him but afterwards when dad had run him home mam said to me...

"Oh he's very nice but it might be better if you get friends like yourself."

Afterwards, I heard them talking.

"I'm worried about him. He only seems able to make friends with simpletons or nig-nogs."

"Thank God that turban's coming off."

The doctor slowly unravels the bandages.

"There you go Mrs Johnson, what do you think?"

Mam looks at me, studying and inspecting my ears. After some time she turns to thank Mr Singh, the surgeon.

"You've got flat ears," she says on the way home.

"You look almost normal now," says dad.

"Still big though," laughs mam.

And I laugh too.

"A Bunny-Girl at 'The Cabaret Club.' I mingled with all the stars: Shirley Bassey, Matt Monroe, Petula Clarke, Dusty Springfield, The Dave Clarke Five, The Tremeloes. I knew them all. It was such a glamorous life."

When I was ten mam told me "a secret." She swore me not to tell anyone because

"If you do you'll break your dad's heart and our marriage would be over."

I never told anyone.

I didn't fuck her because I couldn't get a hard on. I was too drunk and I didn't really fancy her. She had eyes done up like a panda and her name was 'Snoopy.' She was a bit fat. It was just as well because later, another lad, I can't remember his name, fucked her and caught a dose. I sneaked her downstairs in the morning and pretended that she'd spent the night on the settee. Mam gave her breakfast and dad drove her home in silence and then on the way back he went mad with me.

"You ought to be ashamed, bringing sluts like that back home."

It didn't stop when we got back to the house.

"To think that I cooked her breakfast for her, the fat ugly cow."

His name was George and she'd been having an on-off affair with him for years. Simon didn't know and neither did dad.

"I've told you because you are mature and sensitive and you are able to understand."

"Vrrroooom."

"We don't have sex you know. We can't seem to be able to I mean, we've tried, but – well, he can't get it up. I think it's a guilt thing. He feels bad about betraying his wife. But we love each other. I love your dad too, of course I do; it's just that, well, this is different. I shouldn't be telling you this, you're so young and really, it's not your business. It's just that I have to tell someone and I can't tell Simon but I feel I can trust you. It's awful us talking like this behind your dad's back. Your poor dad. You must never, ever say anything to anyone."

I was fifteen and she was thirteen. Kerry was her name. She came to our house in the middle of the night with her friend, Shirley. They threw stones at my bedroom window to wake me up. I got dressed and sneaked downstairs. We walked around the streets until early morning and then sat on a bench. We were just talking. She told me that girls got a hard-on too, only they called it "the urge." A policeman came and told us all to go back home before he took us home and told our parents.

Four-thirty in the morning and she wasn't home yet.

"Come on, don't worry. Go back to bed."

I climbed the stairs back to bed and dad walked back into the living room. I turned to smile at him but his back was to me and he didn't look round. He just kept on going, straight through the door, his shoulders heaving and his head shaking slightly. I didn't go to sleep for ages and after a while I heard dad come up the stairs and go into their bedroom. I didn't move. I stayed still. As still as a statue. Not even breathing. I didn't hear mam come in, but I remember it was light outside and the birds had started singing...I must have fallen asleep then.

I set fire to my brother's hand once. I read somewhere that if you poured paraffin onto something and set light to it, then only the paraffin burned. So I poured paraffin over his hand and set light to it. His hand went up in flames and all I could see was orange and white. I panicked and stuck it under the tap. Fortunately he was okay. I gave him a Mars bar and made him promise not to tell. Another time we pretended that we were circus acrobats. I opened my bedroom window and told Simon that the window-ledge was a tightrope and that he had to walk across it. I lifted him onto the ledge. We didn't know it, but some neighbours across the road could see us and they 'phoned our house. Mam came running into the room and I got a right hiding. Simon was fine.

My dad's car was parked in the driveway. It wasn't locked. We got in and she gave me a blow-job, over my jeans. It was only a pretend blow-job really but it was nice. She pressed her mouth onto me and started humming and it made me hard.

"Mmmmm."

Before we had separate rooms I used to make my brother sleep in the ottoman. Well, I used to persuade him to sleep in the ottoman. We'd play 'vampires' and I'd pretend that the ottoman was a coffin and that it would be a great idea for him to sleep in it. So he'd climb in and sometimes he would fall asleep. Then I'd have the bed all to myself.

We nicked off school and sneaked round to our house. We put the radio on.

"Young girl, get out of my mind, my love for you is way out of line, you better run girl, you're much too young girl."

It was 'The Drifters'.

"Is that what you think about me?"

We put a record on then. It was a Mick Ronson L.P. He was singing a song called, 'Only After Dark.'

"I feel my spirit fly, only after dark."

After that we listened to Mick's version of 'Love Me Tender.' It was better than the Elvis version.

"For my darling I love you, and I always will."

Sometimes I would shut the lid on him.

Round her house: She showed me some playing cards that her dad kept in his drawer. They had dogs on them. Dogs and naked women. Doing stuff. She told me that her dad sometimes bought her underwear. She told me not to tell anyone.

"Do you like these?" she said, lifting up her skirt.

When he wouldn't get in the ottoman we'd have to share the same bed. I'd roll a big blanket up and stick it down the middle of the bed to stop him kicking me in his sleep.

He tries to kick me then so I pick up a rock and throw at his head. He's only stood a foot or so away from me and the rock hits him right in the face and he goes down, crying and bleeding. The crowd in the playground starts cheering then.

"Serves you right you fucking Paki. Now fuck off."

Tjinder kept away from me after that and I felt really bad, but it seemed to be the right thing to do.

We went back to the school once, after we'd left, like we'd seen other former pupils do when we were still at school. They'd come and sit in on the classes. Miss Atkinson would give them a warm welcome and big hugs and they'd all drink tea together, all mature and grown up. Me and Paul Boatman and David Rudge went back and Miss Atkinson said "Oh hello" and told us to sit up at the back of the class. She didn't seem that pleased to see us. After the lesson we were walking around and Mr Lewis caught up with us and told us all it was time we were going. So we went.

"Not even a cup of tea," said David Rudge.

We're on the swings when the man comes over and stands in front of us.
"Get your cock out." He says.
Stephen Pearce is crying but I push the man and he falls back and we run to our bikes. We jump on and pedal like mad. We can hear him behind us shouting and swearing, but he's too fat and too slow and we get away from him.

Her dad comes to our house, banging on the door. Mam and dad are at the pub and me and Craig Smith are drinking Clan Dew in the living room and listening to 'Black Sabbath.' Her dad starts going on about how I got her drunk. He's threatening to hit me. Her mam is trying to calm her dad down. I tell him that it wasn't me, that I hadn't even been with her, that she'd gone off with Mike Patterson and that it was nothing to do with me. Craig comes to the door to see what all the fuss is about.

"Oh, it's the pervert," he says.
I start laughing, despite myself.
"What's so funny?" shouts her dad.
"Have you told your wife about those cards you've got?" I say,
"...and about your daughter's nice new panties?"
He goes all red and his wife looks confused and starts asking him what's going on?
They go then. He seems to be in a bit of a hurry.
"Well, that was a laugh." says Craig.
Good times alright.

160

"The prettiest mam in the world."

"Don't ever tell your dad."

"Don't tell anyone."

We are sitting in the back of John Wilde's car. John didn't have a girlfriend but he was the only one who had a car. John would drive us all about the place all night. 'Driver John' we called him. I've got my hand inside Kerry's pants and a finger inside her. She tells me she wants more. John Wilde is watching through his rear-view mirror.
"Keep your eyes on the road," I tell him.
"And your hands upon the wheel," says Kerry, and we both start laughing.
After a while John asks us if there's anywhere we want to go.
"Anywhere," I say, "I'm not bothered."
"Just keep right on till the end of the road," says Kerry.

I'm sitting next to Paul Boatman in his car.
"Where are we going Paul?"
"I dunno, Where do you want to go?"
"I don't really want to go anywhere Paul. Let's just stay here a while eh."

I'm sitting next to Kerry in dad's car. There's a wet patch on my jeans where her mouth was.
"What shall we do now?"
"I dunno, what do you want to do?"
"I don't really want to do anything Iain. Let's just sit here a while eh."

I'm sitting next to dad in his car. There's a wet patch on the side of his face where he's been crying.
"Where are we going dad?"
Dad says nothing. He just keeps staring straight ahead. Driving.
Vroooom.
I never did say anything. Not about that anyway.
Not to anyone.

Rebecca Lisle

Spends most of her time being a mother, housewife and dog-walker, but, talent and time permitting, is trying to be a good story-teller too. She has published eight books for children and has no wish to grow up.

Toppling Lorna

Rebecca Lisle

I used to keep a diary. This is what I wrote on Saturday 7th September 1962.

Got up late. Nothing much happened. Met the new girl next door. Went to bed early.

This is what I remember.

She was wearing a grey-gauzy sticky-out dress. It was sparkling with sequins although some of them were a bit rusty and sparkled only very dimly. Her pink tights bagged at the knees and the gusset wasn't where it should have been. Her feet were bound into long, dirty ballet shoes; she'd stuffed the toes tight with stiff lavatory paper and they crackled and crunched as she walked on her points, as though she were treading on corn flakes.

Strutting up and down her drive, she looked like a defiant, rather lame heron. She couldn't have missed me peering over the wall at her, but she didn't look at me. She stamped up to her doorstep and sat down on the broken yellow and red tiles on the porch floor to retie the ribbons on her shoes.

"What are you looking at?" she snapped.

"Nothing," I lied.

"Good. I'm private, see. And this drive is private. Royal Ballet."

"Royal Ballet," I repeated mysteriously. "You look like a princess." She didn't, but I guessed it would appeal to her.

"Oh, shit-a-brick, I bloody don't," said the ballerina. "But you'll see, 'cos I bloody will."

Her name was Lorna and her hair was never clean.

My mother didn't mind Lorna's hair being rats' tails dripping down her back, actually, she really seemed to admire Lorna for it.

"Lorna's hair is *absolutely filthy!*" she said to my father.

Absolutely filthy! But she might have been saying, *wonderful!* or *darling!* it was the same tone.

Now we're in October. Friday 25th 1962.

Lorna came for tea and stayed the night. Stayed up talking really late. And I remember her terrible nightie with holes gaping in the seams. It felt nutty, like the inside of a badly cleaned cereal bowl and it was grey from being washed with darks – so my mother told me. She made it sound like a deadly sin; something as bad as the catholic girls in the home across the road might do. Never mix your wash! Watch out for the darks, they'll run! She knows nothing about laundry, that woman, said my mother, pressing the words deep into her crisp white sheets with the hot iron.

Lorna's jumpers were too short, her socks fell down, her knickers were sometimes boys knickers with a special hole at the front. She didn't mind. Lorna could run like a boy, chin forward and pumping arms. And she climbed trees and could swim underwater from one end of the pool to the other.

Lorna didn't have friends at school. The boys laughed at her and the girls despised her. She didn't care:

"What's your name?"

"Lorna."

"Lorna? Lorna what?"

"*Doon* ask me!"

I lived next door to her, right next door so we even shared a wall so we had to be friends.

A new year. There's hardly any mention of what really went on. Here's February 1963.

Rained today. Played with Lorna. Joan was ill, had to play at our house.

When Joan wasn't ill she wore orange lipstick and purple blouses and heavy misshapen beads like old grapes dripped round her neck. But mostly Joan was ill.

Joan was ill in a dark, dangerous way which meant the curtains were drawn and we had to tiptoe and whisper in her house. Dirty glasses sat making dirty rings on tables and dirty plates grew green fungus as they waited for Joan to get better. No meals were cooked unless Lorna made them. Lorna could make a very tasty Welsh rarebit and flat Yorkshire puddings. When Joan was ill she had her meals with us.

When Joan was ill she just wasn't there. I mean she was there, physically, but didn't seem to take up the space she inhabited. Like a phantom. I was forever catching glimpses of her in the shadows of the house; a flash of her dragon dressing gown, a trail of her purple scarf and then nothing. Lorna and I were too scared of her to ever go looking. She wasn't the sort of mother you'd take a couple of aspirin to. She was brittle as a twig and could snap if you closed a door too sharply or wore the wrong shoes. She was the scariest grown-up I ever knew.

Lorna never mentioned it. I waited for her to tell me about it. I wanted to know what went on when I wasn't there, I wanted to know what they talked about, if they did; how Lorna had no clean clothes, how no one cared. I wanted Lorna to *admit* it was awful and she wouldn't. She never, ever did.

On wet Saturday mornings while Lorna's mother was still in bed and mine was busy with the Saturday Morning Chores, we took magazines up to my bedroom and searched for pictures of women modelling underwear; laced-up corsets, elasticated roll-ons or rocket-shaped brassieres. And sometimes, if we were lucky, men in pants...with *bulges*. We cut them all out and put them in shoe boxes and wrote PRIVATE and KEEP OUT on the top.

What I couldn't understand, was that Joan didn't mind in the least, she thought it was funny, she used to encourage us. I don't know what my mother would have thought because I never dared show her.

Saturday 22nd April 1963.

Got up early. Lorna lied. Lorna is such a liar.

Lorna didn't get as much pocket money as me. Sometimes she never got any, not because there wasn't any, but just her mother forgot. Or else

Lorna was paying it back for breaking something, or it wasn't fashionable and she was getting a monthly allowance. Nothing was for certain in the house next door.

We decided to supplement our measly income by taking money from our mothers. It was easy: whenever my mother left her handbag around, I sneaked a few pennies out and we'd soon collected enough for something really decent. But I knew, as I stood looking at the expensive toys in the cabinet at the corner shop, that it was a mistake. I knew from the look in kind Mr Roland's eyes that he knew we shouldn't be there.

"Go on," Lorna urged and I paid for a small stuffed tiger I didn't want.

Lorna bought one too.

We stood outside on the pavement and stared at the useless toys, then at each other.

"My mother will know," I wailed. "Here, you have them both."

But Lorna didn't want them both. "Don't be such a damn soppy thing," she said. "Just fucking lie."

I blushed. I never dared said fuck. And I was no good at lying.

"Where on earth did that come from?" cried my mother when she saw the stupid tiger. "You never had enough money for that! Did you steal it? Where did you get the money? Have you been taking money from my purse?"

Yes. Yes. Yes.

I wept. I cried. I gave my toy to the cleaner's little girl and vowed never to steal again.

My mother told Lorna's mother.

I felt sorry for Lorna because I knew Joan would be so mad, I was all ready to comfort her and let her spend the night in my bed and everything, but then Lorna lied. She dared to deny it. She flatly, absolutely and categorically denied it. If she'd only admitted, just to me, what it was all about, that her mother was a cow, that she hated her, and wished she could come and live in our house, I would have forgiven her everything.

But she didn't. She wouldn't.

"Well, of course I believe my own daughter," said Joan. She eyed my mother coldly over the wall. Her cigarette smoke was blue in the sunlight; her lips a smudge of tangerine. "She says she didn't steal and I believe her."

Lorna and I stared hard at each other; she beside her mother and I beside mine. I mouthed: *I hate you*, to her and then we never spoke about it ever again. And Lorna never owned up. She even got to keep her stuffed tiger.

I didn't realise for years and years that she hadn't owned up because she didn't dare. She was too scared, she knew her mother would have done something truly terrible to her.

Lorna never said *fuck* or *bloody*, or *shit-a-brick*, which was one of her favourites, when she came to our house. She was smart like that. She always helped clear the table after meals and though my mother cringed when Lorna scraped the bits off the plates and stacked them at the table, she never said a word.

Lorna was an overflowing fountain of politeness. Once or twice she nearly curtsied when she came into our house.

"Oh, thanks ever so, Mrs Tappett, you are kind. Are you sure there's enough dinner for me? Do you really? Thank you. Please. Ever so. You are *kind*."

But the best time for Lorna was later, putting on my mother's white apron with the honeysuckle embroidered on the bib and doing the dishes. Especially if my father was doing the drying up. Especially then. And I hated doing the dishes. I hated drying up and so did she, at her house. But listening to my father and Lorna at the kitchen sink you would have thought it was the funniest, jolliest past-time in the world.

Saturday 27th May 1963.

Look at this, I even lied to my diary.

Uncle Paul gave Lorna one whole £1. I think he's horrid. Lorna is really mean.

It wasn't like that.

Uncle Paul was Joan's special friend. He was tall and very thin like a bit of piping and always wore corduroy trousers and ribbed jumpers and he drove a car with no roof. He had once taken LSD and it had made him write poetry and now he could never work again. He gave Lorna a pack of half-pennies from the bank, all wrapped up in an official blue paper bag. Naturally there were 480 of them...until I stole one.

I buried it in the garden. I never owned up to it. Not even to myself. Lorna knew. Uncle Paul knew. But I never told. I dug a little grave for the coin at the bottom of our garden. The soil was hard and crusty. I can smell the sap oozing out of the horse-chestnut tree and see that grey, grey dust that was our garden soil.

Thursday 22nd June 1963.

More lies.

I think Joy Jenkins is a nice girl and I'm going to invite her home for tea. Lorna got a stupid new dress with stupid keys and we aren't talking.

I remember every detail of that dress of Lorna's. It was really crummy. It had a plastic belt with two plastic keys dangling off it and Lorna said they were magic keys and would open a secret box. All the girls wanted to play with Lorna that day and even Mrs McCluskey told Lorna her dress was beautiful.

Nobody noticed my new shiny black shoes.

At playtime I sat on the low wall that divided the boy's playground from ours, swinging my feet in their new shoes. I let Joy Jenkins sit next to me.

"I've got new shoes," I said.

"Oh, yes."

"Don't you like them?"

"Oh, yes."

"Don't you wish you had new shoes like me?"

"Oh, yes."

Oh, shit-a-brick, Joy.

Tuesday 7th December 1963.

I wrote: *Can't wait for the Christmas Play. I want to be Mary. I've never been Mary.* Well at least that was true.

We all wanted to be Mary, even Cecil Baker wanted to be Mary.

I remember how Christmas came whizzing towards us as if sliding along on a sledge. It was so exciting, threatening to crash into us, sending gloriously golden parcels and beribboned boxes exploding into the air. Everything took on an exotic air, the old brass fender, the special silver teapot brought out of its covers, the tissue-wrapped fruit.

Joan didn't believe in Christmas. She didn't believe in Jesus. She said she didn't mind if Lorna wanted to put up decorations, but she wasn't going to. My mother said she was mean-spirited and should do it for her child.

"I'm sorry your mother is mean-spirited," I said to Lorna.

"She isn't. And I don't care about decorations and trees and Christmas. They're old fashioned. Anyway, my mother is a socialist."

"My mother says your mother should do it for you."

"Well your mother is a pig."

Thursday 8th December 1963.

Just a few, well-chosen words.

Lorna is my best friend and I hate her.

I loved Christmas. I wanted Lorna to share it with me. I could have been like Scrooge was after the third ghost visited him and she could have been Bob Cratchett. Only she wouldn't play.

Christmas was so good in those days.

We had cards from people I didn't know and they put ten shilling notes in for me. My parents forgot to send me to bed and time rolled by, up and down the piano keys with carols so sad my throat was perpetually burning with a lump too big and hard to swallow.

It was almost too much: too whizzy, too bright.

And then the Nativity Play.

One night my parents had friends to dinner. I lay in bed listening to their loud voices: the chink of glass and china.

I sneaked downstairs and peeped in at my special Christmas Party mother with her secret cleavage showing and her lips redder than Father Christmas.

Everyone looked hot and shiny. Mouths cavernous and crammed with crashing, gnashing teeth, and so noisy, not like normal at all.

Talk, laugh, talk, laugh.

Then I heard: *nativity play.*

"...yes, that's right," my mother was saying, "and poor little Daisy, she so wanted to be Mary..."

"And what is she?"

"She's a tree!" my mother spluttered.

They laughed so much, I swear they were nearly sick.

I crept away. It was true. I was going to be a tree. I had not been chosen. Again.

December 19 1963.

I hate school. I'm never going back. Lorna is rubbish and so is her mum.

The Nativity Play was not a success.

I didn't say a thing when Mrs McCluskey pushed me into the tube of brown cardboard. I never murmured as the elastic band was pushed onto my head and paper leaves twisted and snagged in my hair. I gritted my teeth while my brown jersey arms were hooked out through either side of the tube.

I was placed at the back of the stage. Scenery, but scenery with staring, murderous eyes which never left Mary.

Mary. Yes, of course, *Lorna* was Mary.

It's only fair, my mother had said. I think it was very kind of Mrs McCluskey to give the part to Lorna. It's what Lorna needs. She hasn't much.

Oh, no! Just a ballet dress. Just a dress with keys. Just getting to eat our dinner and make my father laugh. Just uncles that give her whole pounds in halfpennies. Just an awful mother who goes on ban-the-bomb marches and smokes non-tipped cigarettes…

Life wasn't fair, but still, life went on.

The play started and there I was, standing against a backdrop of distorted cows and sparkling silver-foil stars, stiff and tree-like.

Lorna/Mary held her plastic baby as if it was a pair of precious silk ballet shoes, rocking it, smiling at it.

I knew I was ready to die.

Without warning, my feet began shuffling forward in tiny tree-like footsteps.

"Keep still!" Mrs McCluskey hissed from somewhere in Outer Space. "Daisy, stop!"

I went on shuffling up to the front of the stage, right up to the cardboard manger and the stuffed lambs and cuddly cow. I shuffled up so close I could see the pulled out strands on Joseph's striped towel head-dress. So near I could smell Lorna/Mary. So close that she had to look up at me.

170

Then I flung my branch arms up and roared:

"TIMBER!"

And fell.

Joseph toppled into the three Kings. I smashed into smiling Lorna/Mary and rolled on top of the crib sending the baby Jesus bouncing to the floor.

"Jesus! My baby!" Lorna/Mary cried.

I rolled helplessly across the stage like a giant sausage. One second admiring the cracks in the ceiling, the next the dust on the floor.

At last, the tree trunk rolled to a standstill, my eyes rested on the audience, row upon row of white, startled moons. Joan wasn't even there. She didn't agree with Nativity Plays. But one whiter than white circle was my mother.

I couldn't quite see, was she looking at me, or was she, was she possibly *still* looking at Lorna?

Frank Cossa

Editor's Choice

Frank Cossa, a native of New York City, has won national awards as a playwright and filmmaker, never having studied either. He rarely writes, or even reads, short stories. CLOUD SHADOWS spilled out, unannounced, during a three-month sojourn in Italy. He divides his time between New York and Charleston, South Carolina, where he teaches, writes, plays tennis fitfully, and remains bewildered by almost everything.

Cloud Shadows

Frank Cossa

And so she finds herself again in one of these places. One of these places her father loves. Places teetering on the edges of continents. Landscapes like blanched skeletons, where the nearness of the sea only mocks the parched earth. Unstable places where mountains bestir themselves every hundred years or so to blow smoke plumes at the Sun and leave, where villages had been, stygian rivers of gurgling mud. Sometimes an island that had slipped its moorings, drifted away from an archipelago, and come to rest equidistant from anywhere. More usually it was at the end of a peninsula, an ostentatiously virile incursion into some gulf or channel or strait named for a sixteenth century Portuguese. Sometimes it was an unlikely isthmus separating oceans.

She hated these southern latitudes, where interior and exterior are cleft only by a curtain of beaded strings; where small men the color of copper or of coffee leave baskets of eggplants and melons and, muttering some medieval invocation, refuse to take money. Who ply the coastal waters in barques of such whimsical rigging as to seem able to sail forward and backward at the same time. Men who seem to care only for arcane sports where animals kill each other. She hated the fatalism of people eternally punished by the light; of lives pressed between mountains and the sea. She had been named – *he* had named her – for this unforgiving southern light.

All vows forgotten, Chiara was again in one of these places, where a stout Carthaginian general had once stopped on his way to threaten the Roman Republic. She was here again, for the last time, to say goodbye to her father.

Her mother, known in her wide circle as Kaye, had rung her from some distant airport. "Bring Dan and the kids," she'd said with the high-pitched enthusiasm of the women who sell detergent on television. "We'll make it a whole family...uh...thing."

Chiara did not have quite the heart to point out that, whatever a family *thing* might be, this family was long past having one; that her mother would propose such a journey only if money lay at the end of it.

"Well, there is some paper work," Kaye had confessed after only moderate prodding.

"You mean you want more of dad's money."

"It's not for me dear, It's for you and your family. Think of the kids."

"We don't need, and I really don't want..."

"I want to make sure we get what's coming to us. He'll just leave it to some cockamamie Good Cause, or a young nurse with wicked eyes, and I'll be left without..."

"Mother you have a very comfortable..."

"Somebody has to think about the practical things. *You* certainly don't." This was the moment, as in every phone conversation with her mother, when Chiara considered whether she should scream or hang up, or both, and in what order.

"Besides, the boys will love it. It's a nice spot." Kaye referred to places in the world as "spots," as if ink had splashed on a globe. She had once referred to Indonesia as "not a nice spot."

Even before Kaye deployed the heavy artillery about missing her grandchildren and being a bereft old woman, the battle was lost. Chiara would forego pointing out that Kaye might see more of her grandchildren if she'd remain in one place long enough. That *I Tatti* would somehow stumble along without her presence at their Board Meetings, not to mention the need "since I have to be in Tuscany anyway," to take a villa for a month or two. That the newly excavated caves in Cappadocchia were probably very much like the last batch and would, having lasted this long, still be around next year or the year after. Kaye blamed "your father" for instilling this wanderlust in her but since the divorce she had undertaken these journeys with the excited preparation of a Victorian *memsahib* remembering to order enough *Fortnum and Mason's* marmalade for a three-year sojourn in the Hindu Kush. Kaye's voyages of cultural conquest were made, these days, in the company of sleek young men of no precise employment but who seemed to be very good at making travel arrangements.

The family *thing* went as well as could be expected given the *dramatis personae*. At the first luncheon, sumptuous at a long table on a crumbling terrace, Kaye regaled them with accounts of exotic "spots," fine Colonial hotels where movie stars stayed, and the importance of her work in "conservation." This to no one's surprise led, by the time the fruit arrived, to the "paper work" she required. The boys, unaccustomed to these leisurely southern meals, and having rejected all that was set before them, grew restless. Dan, trooper that he was, offered to take them to the beach and, on the way, find something they would eat. Chiara blushed, head lowered, glancing up at her father just as he glanced at her, reading him as she always had. He was thinking, she knew, that she had bred two more American savages, two more consumers of popular culture without sense or regard.

Days passed this way. Her "paper work" resolved, Kaye went in search of "a decent hotel in this god-forsaken place," and was soon to be found always in the company of two young men of such startling beauty that Chiara actually blinked when she first saw them. They were not employees of the hotel. Their time seemed to be spent entirely in attendance upon Kaye's every need. What they did for a living before her mother arrived here Chiara preferred not to know. She possessed a cracked, sepia toned photo of Kaye, taken perhaps thirty-five years earlier, that had appeared in a newspaper with a caption describing her as a "society beauty," as if this were an occupation. In it Kaye was preposterously attired in jodhpurs and brandishing a riding crop. Preposterous because Chiara knew this woman to be terrified of horses and nervous around all animals. Still she liked to gaze at the picture from time to time and try to imagine the taut, edgy person she knew as the jaunty "society beauty" smiling buoyantly in her silly flaring pants. Chiara wondered how she could have sprung from such narrow loins.

"I never would have had you if I'd known how much it would hurt," Kaye had said to her once. Chiara understood this, even as a tall, broad-boned adolescent, to be merely a statement of fact and not meant personally. Still it was something of a shock to hear that one's mother would have preferred to be something other than one's mother. Only after many more years would Chiara come to see that Kaye's defining characteristic was disappointment. Who else would embark on a *third* round-the-world cruise because the first two failed to produce enough wonders to meet her expectations? Likewise her marriage. Kaye had thought to marry a celebrity but got an artist instead.

With Kaye and her young retinue posed languidly in the hotel lounge and Dan and the boys in whooping exhilaration at the beach, Chiara spent a good deal of time at her father's house. The very same where, years earlier, she had helped him place a sign over the gate, one he had lettered with her help, which read: VILLA DI LAPIDATO. This, though Kaye instantly judged it to be "foolish," was the source of no end of merriment to Chiara and her father. Particularly when the local villagers, taking it to be a family name of ancient lineage, called her "Signorina di Lapidato." And even more so when an earnest young German with a backpack came to inquire about the "Lapidary Museum."

Now not only the sign but the gate too was gone. Chiara made some attempts at reversing the entropy at work in the garden, whereby it would soon return to its natural state as a field of low scrub, but the Sun on her back was too hot. She saw relatively little of her father. He spent the cool hours of the morning "writing" although the sheets of Venetian paper covered with his left-handed scrawl, that she had always transcribed for him with a reverence worthy of the monastic scriptorium, mostly failed to appear. He once wrote a shimmery, watercolor prose, often dedicated to her. His writing now, *when* he wrote, seemed to stumble out of a haze, sodden and disoriented.

They lunched together on the weedy terrace where a green lizard frequently displayed a red throat pouch, whether in a show of ferocity or sexual preparedness they could not tell, and with a grizzled old cat who appeared promptly at meal times but was never seen otherwise. Kaye joined them rarely, objecting to "that little black thing who serves lunch. What's *her* job I wonder? What does he pay *her* for?"

"She's not black, mother."

"Black enough." For Kaye skin tone and moral depravity were closely linked. "It's disgusting. A man of his...his status."

"He *is* divorced, you may recall."

"Nevertheless. Neverthe*less*."

Privately Chiara too wondered about this serious, silent young woman of perhaps Moroccan origin who, like the nameless cat, was seen only at meals, and who might be heard as faint stirrings in the house at other times.

"I always knew when he had his eye on another woman," Kaye said. "You can tell when a man's attention wanders. I just never made a big thing of it. But this, *this* is too much."

Chiara knew better. Kaye had never known anything about the man she'd married. Not his work, not his demons. It had always been the two of them. Chiara and her father off on some giddy enterprise, and Kaye disclaiming all responsibility.

After lunch, when her father retired for his siesta, Chiara, having matched his consumption of *Malvasia,* would read and doze on the terrace, accompanied only by flies and the tirelessly macho lizard. Sometimes, gazing up drowsily from the book was like turning the page. The courtly bowing of the pine trees in the high, elusive breeze, the humming of the flies, the lizard's startling pouch, all became elements in some unsuspecting author's meticulously crafted narrative.

Then, to rouse herself, Chiara would put down the book and have a walk, usually in the direction of the village, higher up the hill, on an unpaved road that exhaled hot dust over her sandalled feet. The streets were deserted at this time of day unless it was a Saint's feast, or school had just let out. Once a red-faced cyclist, in the gaudy livery of one who had taken a disastrously wrong turn in the *Tour de France*, whirred by her on his way, no doubt, to a personal best that no cheering crowd would witness. Another time, as she reached the village, she heard a sudden clatter on the cobbled street behind her and was nearly knocked down by two mounted soldiers, resplendent in sashes and plumes, and prepared every inch, Chiara thought, for World War I. Otherwise, anyone with any sense was resting behind thick walls and tightly latched shutters.

The church was open. Sprawling ungainly and resolute over one end of a convex piazza at the top of a wide flow of travertine steps, its plain white facade almost blinding at midday, its single portal yawned blackly. Chiara was unprepared, as she always was, for the Baroque explosion inside. Segmented arches, broken entablatures, twisting Solomonic columns of porphyry or *cippolino* marble, *trompe l'oeil* angels tumbling through the ceiling, the whole gilded, stuccoed, ecstatic mess of seventeenth century decor trying, it always seemed to her, to plunge and wrench itself free of its homely casement.

There was a crypt. It lay beneath the High Altar and was all that remained of the much older edifice on the site. Chiara hesitated on the steep stairs that led down to it, allowing the musty coolness to play over her like a silk canopy. A group of women, shrouded as if in mourning, sat facing a small altar and were intoning prayers in response to an oddly metallic voice. Not wishing to disturb them Chiara moved quietly across the back of the chapel for a closer look at the remains, encased in glass, of a parish priest who died in 1867 and, according to a nearby plaque, was adjudged by all who knew him to have led a blameless life. Above the low slab of the altar, facing the praying women, was a mosaic, unmistakenly Byzantine, of the Pantocrator: Christ as lawgiver. Not the patient victim invented by Renaissance painters but the harsh judge from an earlier, more forbidding Christianity. The shudder that went through Chiara was from something more than the dankness of the low vaulted room. Something remembered from freezing mornings in school chapels with black-veiled nuns hovering, and her parents far away. A queasy flutter rose to her throat and, simultaneously, slithered down her loins. A brackish sweat poured out of her and she thought she might vomit or have an orgasm right there under the hollow eyes of the dead curate. She was distracted by some acoustical quirk of this ancient space. The voice leading the prayers was coming from just behind her shoulder. For a terrible instant she expected the bony hand of a ferociously hawkish nun to seize and shake her. But it was a loudspeaker affixed to a stone column. It was like the tape-recorded voices of *muezzins* she had heard calling the faithful to prayer from any number of minarets in more exotic places than this.

Chiara did not so much leave as flee the church. Even the buzzsaw light outside was preferable to the dizzying, incense-sweetened coolness within. A small woman, probably younger than she looked, followed her outside and accosted her on the steps. In her hand she held out a small, rough object. The woman spoke rapidly in an almost impenetrable dialect but Chiara understood the word for "pregnant" repeated several times. Then she recognized the thing in the woman's hand. A miniature penis. For an instant she thought it was a relic, removed perhaps from the well-preserved cadaver of the virtuous priest in the crypt, who had little use for it even in life. On taking it from the woman she saw that it was fashioned crudely of wax. The woman made her to understand that if she had it blessed by a priest, and left it as an offering in the church, *La Madonna* would take pity on her barrenness and bless her with a child. Although Chiara could speak the language well enough, it was too much trouble to explain that she was far from barren, and actually took steps to insure that she would have no more children, the blessings of *La Madonna* not withstanding. She smiled and thanked the woman and took the penis. Only on closer inspection did she see that it was in fact a gigantic one given the diminutive figure of a man to which it was attached. She recognized the leering visage of *Priapus*. An ancient pagan fertility symbol was now in the service of the Church! Apparently two-thousand years of priests had not entirely banished the old gods. And there was no telling what still lurked in the cloud shadows; what lived on in the long memories of childless women.

As they lunched alone together Chiara listened as her father talked brightly about a new "film project," or an article he felt obliged to dash off to straighten out some knuckleheaded scholar's misapprehension of Orcagna's *Strozzi Altarpiece*. She studied him as she had always. Receiving his likeness, his mannerisms of gesture and inflection, not only through her eyes and ears but almost through her skin. He had come to resemble the very ruins they had travelled so far, so often, to see. The deep lines in his forehead were not merely rolling horizons now but were cut vertically as well like the rusticated masonry of a crumbling *castello*, gouged by winds and chance. The gorge between his eyes gave him the furious aspect of Moses about to smash the Tablets. Thin wisps of silvery hair stirred in even the faintest breeze and came to rest in unexpected configurations. His strong hands, that could go *mano a mano* with Beethoven or a Middleweight Contender, now shook sometimes.

She and her mother had followed this man on some of the most unpromising of itineraries until Kaye grew tired of it. Then it was the two of them. As fast as Kaye would drop her at some Swiss school or other, so would her father swoop, seemingly from the top of the nearest Alp, to rescue her. She never asked where they were going. They were going *away*. Nor was she protected in these foreign destinations. They lived as the people lived. They drank the water. By the time she was ten she'd been through diseases her better-educated schoolmates could not hope to spell, let alone survive.

She'd been happy in one school only, where she'd fallen in love with young, spirited, Sister Angelique, and determined to enter the Ursuline Novitiate as soon as she was old enough. When her father visited she brought her two great loves together and skipped happily beside them as they walked in the cloister chatting about her academic progress. Then, in an instant, her life was changed forever. She saw Sister Angelique look at her father not in the neutral way that nuns regarded the world but as a woman gazes longingly at a man. It was not much more than a glance. Her father missed it completely. But Chiara saw it and wanted to yank Sister Angelique to the ground by her wimple and pummel her with fists and knees. How dare she? How, even for an instant, even unconsciously, *dare* she?

Chiara spoke to Sister Angelique after that only to give formal, scrupulously correct, answers in class. The nun too grew serious, and then sad. By the end of term Chiara had convinced her father that she hated the school and changed her mind about a religious vocation. She left without saying goodbye. Occasionally she still wondered what ever became of Sister Angelique. She even thought of writing to thank her for completing her education so succinctly that day; for teaching her the most important thing she ever learned. *We are all made of the same stuff.* It became a kind of mantra for her.

In the evenings she would coax him out for a walk, to look at the sea or the mountains, to find a place to drink an *aperitivo*, to watch the light change colors on peeling, stuccoed walls. Much about him annoyed her. His quick irritability at the slightest disruption of his internal schedule, his tendency to mumble and then become cross when no one heard him, his frequent skirmishes with inanimate objects – unable as he was to manage any machine more complicated than a toaster. Such quirks as had seemed, when she was young, the eccentricities of a lofty mind, now appeared peevish and self-indulgent. His facility with languages she'd always found alarming. He could so easily slip away from her and Kaye by slipping into another tongue, like an actor donning a costume and a different personality with it. One smirking aside to a hotel porter, in Senegalese, and he was gone.

He had been a promising writer, then a promising filmmaker. He'd appeared on critics' lists of *Ten Best*...or *Twenty Most...*, he'd been interviewed on Public Television. Then not. He became one of those cranky intellectuals people see at gallery openings and storefront theatres. People remembered his name but not why they remembered it. He had, it was true, once made a film of spare and searing beauty that still turned up at the sort of Festivals held in the Massif Centrale in February.

There came the wanderings with wife and daughter, and then, when Kaye peeled off to reclaim what she could of her career as a "society beauty," with daughter only. There was always a "project" at the end of these travels, some essential piece of research only he could accomplish. But for one whose work and manner dealt almost exclusively with the ironic, he never saw the irony in his quest for recognition in places so removed from the great centers. Even his young daughter could see before too long that this Grail he sought was really not likely to turn up during a visiting lectureship at the University of Dakar.

And even she would leave him. She could just remember the moment.

In some teeming bazaar, brilliant with mounds of spices and plastic soccer balls, a new but familiar scent, or maybe a surprising light on a piece of fabric hung out to dry, set off something she had never felt. Like a migratory bird she knew it was time to fly north. Having never made this journey alone before she had no idea how long it would be nor how she would know where to stop.

For a time he followed *her*. Her power to summon him was Chiara's introduction to the possible, to what could be done in the world. That he would leave wherever he was, leave whatever actress he was "seeing" at the time, and come to her, explained everything. Then came a more conventional education, jobs, husband and children, in which her father took no interest. She employed all the latest gadgets produced by the Age of Communication but his voice grew ever fainter. Finally it faded completely into the din of real life. Only occasionally did that voice whisper to her. Once, at yet another Christmas party, holding yet another glass of *Beaujolais nouveau,* looking at her hosts' bookshelves of Metropolitan Museum catalogues and pre-Columbian artefacts, she was struck by a fit of laughter so debilitating she had to be taken home.

The family *thing* ended when Kaye declared it time to go. An endangered temple on the Anatolian coast required her immediate attention. With her two young Atlantids laboring under her luggage, she bestowed hasty air-kisses on everyone and was off in a sputtering taxi. Chiara hugged her father, and joined Dan and the boys for the long drive to the nearest city with an airport. Her sons were delighted to get back home in time for the playoffs," and noisily debated the ramifications of "wild cards" and "home field advantage." Dan was stalwart in respect of Chiara's silence.

She lasted until their flight was announced. "I have to go back," she said to Dan. "I can't leave him like this."

"Go," Dan said, having heard much, and supposed more, about Chiara's father, "I'll explain it to the boys."

Chiara thought through it on the winding drive back. What was she, after all, that he had not made her? He'd given her left-handed pencils! When Kaye had bemoaned her *"gaucherie,"* and her copybook letters were so tipsy they threatened to fall over, he'd provided a handful of "specially designed pencils for those rare and gifted individuals who operate *a sinistra*." And her schoolgirl penmanship did straighten up a bit. She attributed the currently illegible state of her writing to the appalling dearth of left-handed pencils in the United States. She still treasured the lefty catcher's mitt he'd bought her, and was convinced that she would be a famous photographer if anyone had sense enough to make a left-handed camera.

And he'd made her hit tennis balls. Long after twilight, when her hand was raw and she could barely see the ball through the salt brine in her eyes, and she begged to stop, he'd say "a few more," and "winners don't cry when they're hurt, they get mad." The first time she was able to beat him in a set, he'd muttered something about a sore ankle, touched her hair, bought her an ice-cream cone.

She had not become a great left-handed tennis player although, for a time, they'd terrorised the club circuit as the most unremitting of mixed-doubles teams. She *had* become a very good left-handed scenic designer who hardly ever cried. She was a winner, was she not? Was she not, even after two pregnancies, lean and swift? Was she not the one they all fell in love with, the one longed for, the one missed? And, oh yes, the one who got mad?

She arrived quite late, exhausted by dark, swerving roads. She found him seated at his desk with a half-empty wine bottle, and not much more than a candle for light. He let her stand there in the doorway until he finished the sentence he was writing. Then he looked up at her, unsurprised.

"Forget something?" he said, as if she'd been gone for a few minutes.

"You came here to die." She took his lack of response for an affirmative. "Heart?" A nod this time. "Ever hear of bypass surgery?"

"Bypassed long ago. Not enough left to patch together." A pause. "Was there anything else?"

"Your Moroccan can't be good for your heart."

"Tunisian, and nothing to do with my heart. Only you."

"Dad, don't."

"You left me."

"I couldn't be just an extension of you. I had to find a life."

"Appointments? Deadlines? *Traffic?*"

She let the expected sarcasm float away harmlessly. "Could we have just gone on? As we were?"

"Why not?"

"Why *not?* For god's sake! Do you feel nothing about…all that?"

"All *that?* You used to have a better vocabulary."

"I was a child."

"You were never a child."

"If I'd done the same thing with a boyfriend you'd have said I was too young."

"Yes."

"Different rules for you."

"For *us*, yes. You understood then."

"Understood? I was sixteen."

"Then you were eighteen, then you were twenty."

"By then it was…"

"When I came to visit you at college *you* made the hotel arrangements, *you* booked adjoining rooms."

She let the darkness absorb this. She had done that, and with a quiver in her bowels that she felt again whenever she thought of it. That she felt again even now.

"Did you come back to blame me?"

"No."

"Forgive me?"

"No."

"What then? Proclaim your status as a victim? Revise your memoirs to suit your current view of yourself? Don't expect my *imprimatur*."

"Don't you care about the *damage?* How long it took to recover from you?"

His eyes quizzed upwards like a scolded child's. "I created you. You're what I'll leave behind. My *capolavoro*. When I'm gone you'll have all there ever was of me. Unshared by anyone. Who else could give you that. Who *would?*"

He looked, in this dismal light, beautiful and hurt like the last player in a boyish game of *snap-the-whip* who had been thrown by centrifugal force and come to rest, a pile of bruised limbs, nowhere near anybody. She knew, as she had known from the beginning, that their love was a theological argument flung onto a Baroque ceiling; layer upon layer of allegory so fraught with emblem and internal reference as to fold in upon itself, so defiant of perspective, of gravity, of the rules of small imaginations, as to require in the end only surrender.

She went and sat across from him, as she had sat across so many restaurant tables with candlelight refracting through half-empty wine bottles in the days when she smiled for him and shook out her hair for him. Now she reached and took his large, slightly shaking hand in both of hers, and held it to her lips and then her forehead in a kind of reverse blessing.

"Send away your Tunisian. I'll stay with you if you want me to."

"Goes without saying."

"No. Say it."

"I want you to stay with me. It's all I've ever wanted."

"I won't be good for your heart."

"Oh, yes you will."

Chiara could see that she too had come to rest, at the end of a thoughtless, whirling, game, in this last of all places, where the difference between interior and exterior is described by a beaded curtain, and small men leave eggplants and melons outside and refuse to take money.

<u>Pansy Billingsly</u>

Winner of the Fish *Short* Short Story

competition (Southhampton Writers'

Conference)

Headline News

Pansy Billingsly

The news had always been part of George's life.

"Don't believe everything you see on TV," his mother used to say. She was the first to warn him of the danger.

"Truth, justice and the American way." George always answered in threes.

And he believed.

Nixon might lie to the American people, but who could doubt Walter Cronkite. Science might fail as it did with the Challenger explosion but who could question the tears in David Brinkley's eyes as he reported it.

George grew up, became a man and married. He loved Judith and meant it to last forever.

"You love Diane Sawyer more than you love me," Judith said one night standing between George and the television set.

"Diane, divorce, disaster," George replied. He liked the alliteration.

"You see nothing but disasters," Judith said. "It's making you weird and paranoid."

"Paranoia, palimony and politics," George said, looking around Judith to see the set.

George watched as the Berlin Wall fell, as the USSR crumbled and as Apartheid died. He couldn't resist the news and Judith threw him out, got a divorce and George's world got smaller. He got an apartment near his job and continued as before. Working, sleeping and watching news.

He'd not heard till nearly noon about the early morning bombing in Oklahoma City because he was at work. He was sleeping when Diana died. It had been hours before he knew. News happened all the time and he missed so much.

It was Tuesday when he decided. "Quit, quake, queen," he told his boss and at the end of the day he was carefully hurrying home from work for the last time. He hugged the walls and widely skirted the gaping alley openings in the three blocks that separated his apartment building from his work place. His path was staggering and odd but George didn't care. It was his routine – his way of avoiding danger on the trip home.

"Muggers, mice and madness. Terrorist, tornadoes and trucks," he repeated as he curved and swayed on his way. A stranger might have thought him drunk, might have missed the pattern of his path. George didn't care about this either. All he cared about was reaching the safety of his apartment one last time. He lowered his head and focused on the pebbly grey of the sidewalk and said, "Anthrax, arson and angina. Bats, bandits and bacteria," to refocus his attention as he hurried on toward safety.

The door was triple locked and it took a few seconds for George to get inside. When he did, he re-locked the door and slumped back against it with relief. The apartment was dark, it had a peculiar door, closed and tomblike. Stale. Light from the television blinked and danced around the walls, the low hum of voices came from the living room. He hung up his coat, went to the kitchen and popped a Healthy Choice turkey and dressing frozen dinner into the microwave, punched in six minutes and hurried to the living room.

It was just as he left it. CNN cast its light against the shadows of the walls. George picked up the remote and flicked through CBS, ABC and NBC. It was 6:30, the witching hour and the news was on each channel. Dan Rather was in Washington, the Capitol Dome over his right shoulder. Tom Brokaw and Peter Jennings reported in front of a bank of television monitors that flickered and danced with George couldn't quite see what.

George sunk into his easy chair and sighed. The news never

188

stopped. It never stopped and George now thought of the men and women who reported it as his family and friends. He liked some of them better than others. Judith had been right. Diane Sawyer was his favourite. She looked so fresh and clean and her words were always crisp and clear. She was the standard he used for all the younger women reporters and without exception they came up short.

George pulled off his shoes and propped his weary feet on the footstool while Tom Brokaw slurred his thin-lipped way into his lead story.

"Starvation, infection and dehydration are listed on thirty percent of the death certificates for residents of a nursing home in Packard, California raising questions about the quality of care Medicare dollars are buying."

"Starvation, infection and dehydration," George repeated.

Images of alligator-skinned people flashed on the screen. They were alive, but barely so, propped in wheelchairs and lining institutional walls. It was sad. George's microwave buzzed and he left the nursing home tragedy long enough to collect his dinner and a beer, returned to his chair and flipped to Peter Jennings.

George thought Peter looked like Tom's younger brother. He also believed Peter shared Mary Albert's sexual proclivities and possibly his women. He forked dressing into his mouth as Peter said, "Larry Flint's triumphant return to Cincinnati brought out fans and protesters today. Flint autographed copies of his best-selling autobiography and Hustler Magazine."

Flint, in his wheelchair, looked used up to George, much like the nursing home residents in Tom's lead story. The camera panned the magazines Larry was signing – a red cover with a splay legged woman. George leaned forward and focused on the cover, but the image changed before he could really *see* the cover.

He had a forkful of turkey, chewed without tasting and flipped to CBS. Dan Rather was reporting on presidential campaign funding and Ronald Reagan was on the screen. A mix of old and news. George snickered. "Funding, famine and Flint." he said.

When seven came, he flipped back to CNN and watched till way past bedtime. He could do that now, with no boring job to go to in the morning. George had worked as a security guard – on his feet, watching black and white screens for signs of trouble. Boring people going about their boring business in one boring building. In thirty minutes the network news took him to California, Ohio and Washington and spanned the years from 1982 to 1997. The news was large. George thought it was the largest and now he could spend his waking life watching something that mattered, being where the action was.

"Largest, labor, latchkey," George whispered before he slipped off to sleep.

He heard about and saw teenagers killing one another from coast to coast. The latest gang in Pearl, Mississippi who were scaring folks who'd already seen everything. George could see the fear in their eyes as they spoke into the cameras.

George saw paedophiles, policemen and politicians. Rodman, Rosie and rapists. Famines, floods and mudslides. Not everything could be properly grouped, no matter how hard he tried.

George hadn't left his apartment for seven days, told day from night by the tint of the flickers on his wall. He was fascinated, frantic and a little bit frightened at the prospect of going out. That's where the news happened. Out there and he was safe inside, watching but not a part of it. He decided not to go, even when his beer ran out.

With each newscast George's world expanded to troubles that would have broken Job and then shrunk again till he felt he was inhabiting the only place where a whiff of safety still existed. The smallest space possible. The space where he stood, and George had begun to suspect even that but he decided to defend it vigorously.

He pulled his hunting rifle from the closet and rummaged till he found a box of shells. He carried them to the apartment window that faced the street, four stories down. He was furtive and appeared more so in the colored lights reflected from the television set. The news was out there and he felt he had to stop it.

"Veni, vidi, vici," George said and with a decisive thrust he rammed

190

the rifle barrel through the window and began to fire. The Rapid cams arrived before the cops and when it was over George lay on the pavement, beaten, broken and bloody. Dead. The cameras whirred and images of George flickered off the walls of his empty apartment till much later a young cop, head shaking in dismay, punched the off button.

Initial short list

Alison Maxwell

Barbara F. Lefcowitz

Bill Lamp

Bonnie McCune

C. W. Bryant

Catherine Keal

Catherine Noonan

Christina Pacosz

Clarrie Pringle

Dianne Gray

Dorothy Schwarz

Gaynor Arnold

Graham P. Stanford

Gregory Norris

Harry Groome

Helen Bell

Ian Baker

Jane Eaton Hamilton

Jane Griffiths

Jane Heather

Jane Wenham-Jones

Jean Rogers

Joanna Broome

Judith Moore McGinn

Kara Schaff

Kenneth Neil Bell

Kevin Cassidy

Liam McGinley

Linda Parker

Lindsay Hawdon

Loretta Cobb

Marjorie Kowalski Cole

Maxine Alterio

Michael Faber

Mimi Moriarty

Norrie Egan

Owen Ryan

Paul Curley

Pauline McNamee

R. N. Allan

Rhodri Clark

Robert Bell

Roger DeBeers

S. Pandit

Samantha Howard

Samuel Jeremiah Snoek

Sarah Bower

Sharon Bangert Corcoran

Tom Bryan

Final short list

Andrew Heath

Ann Jolly

Bernadette Higgins

Carolyn Lewis

David Farn

Dennis Must

G. E. Campbell

Geona Edwards

Gillman Noonan

He Chunxiao

Heather Doran Barbieri

Jenny Roche Conroy

Julia Widdows

Kieran Byrne

Kieran Murphy

Kristin Jensen

Leo Baltholomew

Linda Thompson

Linnet van Tinteren

Lynn Sadler

Mercedes Lawry

Neil Banks

Penny J. Cotton

Rachel Seiffert

Rob Richardson

Ronan Wilson

Sarah Weir

Sean Murphy

Sue Wood

Sylvia G. Pearson

First Prize :
£1,000 (approx $1,200)

Second Prizes (to be awarded to the two second-best stories) :
– One week at Anam Cara Writers' and Artists' Retreat.
    Contact: Sue Booth-Forbes.
Address: Eyeries, The Beara Peninsula, Co. Cork, Ireland.
Tel: 00 353 (0)27 74441
E Mail: anamcararetreat@eircom.net
Website: www.ugr.com/anamcararetreat/
Situated in one of the most rugged and beautiful parts of Ireland
overlooking Kenmare Bay, this is an ideal place to write. Also to walk,
swim, fish, read, or take a drink in the pubs of the idyllic town of
Eyeries. It is run by Sue Booth-Forbes, who lends a personal touch to
this unique set-up.

– A weekend residential writing course from the Dingle Writing
    Courses 2001 Programme.
Contact: Nicholas McLachlan or Abigail Joffe.
Address: Dingle Writing Courses Ltd, Ballintlea, Ventry, Co. Kerry,
Ireland.
Tel: 00 353 (0)66 91 59052
E mail: dinglewc@iol.ie
Website: www.iol.ie/~dinglewc
On the stunning Dingle Peninsula in Co. Kerry, overlooking the
magnificent Inch Beach, a few miles from the town of Dingle, the
courses here are much sought after. Tutors have included novelists
Jennifer Johnston, Anne Enright, theatre director David Byrne,
playwright Vincent Woods, and poets Pat Boran, Paul Durcan, and
Graham Mort.

Fish Publishing Annual Short Story Prize

£1,000 for the overall winner.

Second Prizes:
week at Anam Cara Writers' Retreat,
weekend writing course

Top 15 stories will be published in Fish's next anthology.

Judges:
Antonia Logue. Others to be appointed.

Conditions:
- Stories must not exceed 5,000 words. There is no minimum.
- Name and address should not appear on text, but on a separate sheet.
- A fee of £8 for the first story is required, £5.00 per subsequent story. £5.00 per story for full-time students, pensioners and the unemployed. Cheques payable to Fish Publishing.
- The judges' verdict is final. No correspondence will be entered into once work has been submitted.
- If receipt of entry, notification of results, or any other information is needed it is necessary to include a SAE or e mail address. Stories will not be returned.
- **Closing date 30th Nov., every year.**
- Results announced 17th March on our website.
- Stories must not have been published previously.
- Entry will be deemed as acceptance of these conditions.
- No entry form is needed.

Critique:
For a fee of £30 a considered critique of your story is available (min 250 words)

Send stories to:-
Fish Short Story Prize
Durrus, Bantry, Co. Cork, Ireland.

fishpublishing@eircom.net   www.fishpublishing.com

Honorary Patrons: *Roddy Doyle, Dermot Healy, Frank McCourt*